THAT FRENCH WOMAN

THAT FRENCH WOMAN

JOSEPH HILTON

CUTTING EDGE

ISBN-13: 978-1-970848-05-2

Published by
Cutting Edge Books
PO Box 8212
Calabasas, CA 91372
www.cuttingedgebooks.com

CHAPTER ONE

F ROM THE COLUMNS of the New York Times:
"Virgin islands, May 12—Mrs. Marie Courcel Boardman,
of Old Haven and New York society, today obtained a divorce
from Winthrop Alden Boardman, Wall Street broker and sports-
man. Mrs. Boardman, a native of France, first married ..."

During the dazzling decade of the 1920's, when money alone was
sufficient to open almost any door, the Maison d'Or remained
the most exclusive as well as the most costly brothel in Paris.

The discreet and highly conventional owners of the establishment were zealous guardians of the reputation carefully
acquired since the turn of the century; they had no intention of
changing simply because the times had changed. Other de luxe
and world-famous bagnios, such as the House of All Nations and
the Crystal Palace, once the nocturnal playgrounds of royalty
or properly introduced gentlemen of finance, might now throw
wide their portals to anyone carrying a sufficiently well-stuffed
wallet. By preference one filled with American dollars. But not
the Maison d'Or.

The latter remained what it had always been—an almost private club catering to a select clientele accustomed to the very best
that life had to offer.

It was justifiably famous for its inmates. Unlike the House of
All Nations, which lived up to its name by recruiting its talent on
an international basis ranging from the fragile tea-rose beauties

of the Orient through the ebony darkness of Africa to the cool Scandinavian contrast of Baltic maidens, or the Crystal Palace, which specialized in more exotic entertainment, the Maison d'Or confined itself to quality.

The girls fortunate enough to be employed there were first of all ladies, in the almost forgotten meaning of the term. An attractive face and body, together with a flair for mechanical passion, were not enough to gain a place on the resident staff or even on the fairly long waiting list. Such girls could be found in any of a hundred houses of tolerance in Paris—or for that matter on any of a thousand street corners after dark.

The Maison d'Or required other talents besides the obvious ones. In more ways than one the place was like a select finishing school, where skill in the social arts and graces and drawing-room comportment was a necessary requisite to advancement. For one of the major roles of the young ladies who made their careers behind the guarded doors of the house on the rue Litre was to make the clients forget that they were patronizing the oldest profession in the world and paying cash on the line, creating instead the illusion of an intimacy based solely on charm and worldly understanding.

It was in the Maison d'Or that Winthrop Boardman first met the girl who called herself Yvonne.

It was Boardman's first visit to the place and he hadn't gone there through design or desire. It was the aftermath of a farewell party for Larry Brewster and Ted Stover, who were sailing back to the States the following day. They had had a long dinner together at the Tour d'Argent and then had made a tour of Montmartre. But it was summer and such spots as Zelli's, the Florida, and Chez Florence were overflowing with American collegiates making the astounding discovery that a ten-dollar express check would buy some 400 francs and that 400 francs in turn would purchase an impressive number of drinks and even more attention from the perambulating prostitutes who made the bars a happy and lucrative hunting ground.

Possibly it was an association of ideas that prompted Larry to make his suggestion.

"Let's get the hell out of this mob and go to a decent place. How about the Maison d'Or?"

Stover let out a doubtful whistle and said, "It's a welcome idea. But from what I've always heard you need a letter from the Prince of Wales or somebody like him to get in the damned place."

"Not me, my friend. My old man gave me a note of introduction along with a letter of credit the first time I came over. Told me that if I was going to raise hell I should do it like a gentleman. Never did tell me how *he* happened to be a favored client, though."

Boardman was of two minds about begging off. He had heard stories about the Maison d'Or and the remarkable beauty and charm of its youthful courtesans and was naturally curious. On the other hand, he had no particular urge for an hour or two of purchased passion.

Helen Avery, the girl to whom he was engaged and because of whom he was in Europe, was still very much on his mind. She and her mother were gradually becoming a perplexing problem.

In the end he decided it was easier to follow along with Brewster and Ted Stover rather than argue the matter.

In spite of his disinterest he was mildly impressed by the formality of the place. There was nothing about the exterior of the house to indicate what went on behind its heavily draped windows. The massive outer doors were opened by a butler who took the card that Larry offered and left them standing in the small vestibule. A brief moment later he returned with an apology for having kept them waiting, took their hats, and ushered them into a reception room at the left of the entrance hall.

From appearance it might have been the drawing room of a well-to-do family with more than the average amount of taste. That same feeling of being in a private home grew on Boardman when a thin, middle-aged woman with white hair came into the room.

Instinctively he stood up, and Larry introduced her as Madame Romain. He was aware of shrewd black eyes appraising him sharply as she waved him back into his chair. Oddly, he was reminded of his college days when the family of some girl he was dating for the first time always found an excuse to look him over when he called for their daughter.

He was vaguely relieved when Madame Romain turned her attention back to Larry.

Her English was only faintly accented as she spoke in a tone of mock reproof.

"You really should have telephoned in advance, m'sieu. Particularly if you had some one special in mind.

"You mean Nicole is busy?"

"By good fortune she is without prior engagements." By her rewording Madame Romain somehow managed to suggest that such engagements as Nicole might have were those of any popular young lady of fashion. "You have the luck of the young and impetuous."

"Americans are always lucky," Larry told her. "Hadn't you heard? And how about my friends here?"

Madame Romain let the latter question hang in the air. Instead of a direct answer she stood up and suggested, "Suppose we join some of the young ladies in one of the private rooms."

She led the way through French doors and along a narrow hallway to a smaller, more intimately furnished drawing room.

Boardman was aware of the murmur of soft voices before he stepped through the doorway. And when he did cross the threshold he stopped short in momentary confusion, certain the whole thing must be an elaborate and fantastic joke.

For the half-dozen young girls grouped about the room definitely could never be suspected of being professional demimondaines. On the contrary, they seemed more like exceptionally beautiful and well-poised debutantes waiting for their escorts to carry them to a ballroom or the theatre. All were in evening dress, and even to Boardman's untutored masculine eye it was obvious that the dresses were expensive and designed by an artist. They acknowledged the introductions pleasantly. A maid appeared with glasses of champagne.

The whole business became increasingly unreal for Boardman. In part he put it down to the considerable amount of drinking he had done that evening. But at the same time he came to grudging realization that it was also due to his own previous misconceptions. He had made up his mind in advance that a brothel was a brothel no matter how fancy its setting or how famous its reputation. What he knew about such places was secondhand, pure hearsay. During his college years he had followed the set pattern of his own crowd. That meant taking out some chorus girl whenever a new musical comedy opened in Boston and trying to arrange a temporary liaison. Once he had had a prolonged affair with an Italian waitress who worked in one of the restaurants near Harvard Square. Handled in that manner you could always boast to yourself that you had made a conquest on your own merits; although, in the long run, such affairs usually ran into a considerable amount of money spent on gifts and discreet outings.

Still, it wasn't like purchasing a woman's favor outright.

He became aware that the girl seated at his side was talking softly and smoothly, murmuring something about Paris in the summer and the theatre and the races.

"I'm sorry," he half apologized. "For the moment I was thinking of something else."

She nodded as if it were a natural thing and then surprised him by suggesting quite naturally, "You were looking at the other girls, perhaps? Is there one in particular that you would care to have join us?"

He made a quick gesture of denial. "I wasn't looking at anyone. It was just that I—that my mind was somewhere else."

Her laugh had an overtone of mocking amusement. "You are quite honest, at any rate, even if not exactly complimentary. But you are certain that there is not one of the others who attracts you more? You have only to make known your choice...."

Again Boardman shook his head negatively. "To tell you the truth, I hadn't noticed any of the others."

Now for the first time he took a full look at the girl beside him, the girl who called herself Yvonne. Her eyes were a blue that seemed to merge into deep violet. Her coal-black hair was simply arranged, parted in the center and caught up at the back in some kind of a Psyche knot. With her slender throat and bare shoulders and partially revealed breasts rising out of the pale-green silk and tulle of her evening gown, she vaguely reminded Boardman of a classical portrait he had once seen hanging in some Back Bay home. Such make-up as she wore was too artfully applied to be noticed, at marked variance from the blatant lipstick and rouge flaunted by the well brought-up girls Boardman knew at home.

There was the sound of voices and laughter across the room and Boardman glanced up. Brewster was just disappearing through the doorway with Nicole, while Ted Stover was making a noisy game out of trying to decide which of the two girls he held by the arms would be his final choice.

Boardman supposed he should make some move himself. He still had no strong desire to avail himself of the hospitality of the house. But on the other hand it would be damned awkward to just go on sitting there like a country lout.

Irritably he wished he could stop thinking about Helen Avery for the moment. He would have an uncomfortable time if any questions were asked as to how he had spent this evening when he had luncheon at Prunier's tomorrow with Helen and her mother. He wasn't any good at casual lies....

Yvonne touched his wrist lightly with her fingertips.

"Suppose we go up to my rooms. You can relax a bit more comfortably there. I think, my friend, that you have had a long day that has left you a little weary."

She might be a damned mind reader, Boardman thought as he followed her up the wide curving staircase. Or maybe she was merely being politely tactful. Whichever it might be, it was a welcome change. All the girls he knew were blunt and outspoken, rarely losing an opportunity to put a man at a disadvantage. It was what the older people at home called the "Flapper Age," blaming it on the war.

Her rooms were on the second floor, consisting of a boudoir-sitting room and a bedroom that could be seen through a half-opened door. She motioned him into an overstuffed easy chair, moved a silver and crystal ash tray into a more convenient position, and pulled at a silken cord.

A moment later the maid who had served them downstairs entered with a silver ice bucket from which the swollen, golden-foil heads of champagne bottles protruded. Boardman watched as Yvonne extracted a bottle, wrapped it in a linen napkin and deftly removed the wire cage beneath the foil, easing the cork gently out with a firm pressure of her thumbs. She poured a minute portion into her own glass first to remove any possible corkage, then filled Boardman's glass before completing her own.

"It is a good year," she advised him, holding up her glass in a silent toast. "1907. Madame was fortunate in laying in a large supply. She is very clever at that sort of thing."

Boardman nodded. Again he was assailed by the incongruity of the evening. It made no sense that he should feel ill at ease just because he wasn't in the mood for following the example of Brewster and Stover. There was no need for him to explain; he owed the girl nothing. After all, she was just a common tart when you came right down to it. Well, maybe not so common, but a tart nevertheless.

Yet when he spoke he found himself half apologizing again. "I'm sorry, but I don't seem to be very gay company this evening."

She smiled at him.

"You are company, m'sieu, and it is not required of you that you be gay. Only that you be at ease and enjoy yourself."

"And if I just want to sit here and talk?"

"But why not? That, too, is pleasant at times. Perhaps you could tell me something about America. Everything I hear about your country only confuses me the more."

Boardman found himself laughing for the first time. "Maybe that's because we're confused ourselves, with too many things happening too quickly. I have a much better idea. Suppose you tell me about yourself."

"There is nothing to tell."

"But there must be." He paused, groping in his mind for the right words to express what had puzzled him from the moment he met her. "I mean—after all, you're here in this place. And it isn't as though you were an ordinary girl."

"Thank you, m'sieu."

"I'm not joking. You know perfectly well what I mean. You've got background and breeding and education. A blind man could see that. Hell, you even speak English better than I do, even if you do have an accent. There must be some damn good reason you came to be in a place like this."

She stared down at the empty champagne glass, twirling it between her fingertips. It was a question that had been asked often, and she usually answered with a story she had told so many times that now it almost rang true to her own ears. Aristocratic parents that had died during the war and family estates that had been lost. A younger sister to support in a convent school in the south of France. The need for money....

Yet tonight, for some reason, she didn't feel like repeating the weary fiction. Possibly because it was an odd evening anyway, what with the strange American she would likely never see again.

There was no need for pretense. For once she could allow herself the relaxation of truth.

"I had no education, *mon ami*," she began softly. "I was born on a farm in Normandy. A very poor and miserable farm and I was a very poor and miserable girl...."

CHAPTER TWO

T HE TOWN WAS Laverny, a few miles from Vernon. A typical small Normandy village of about fifty stone and plaster houses, an ancient church, a grist mill long since fallen into disuse, and a single *bistro* with the usual small zinc bar.

In the same building that housed the *bistro,* there was a store that carried a few staple items, but most of the farmers chose to wait until they carried their produce to the markets in Vernon. Things could be bought a few centimes cheaper there.

Remembering the town, Yvonne could remember only ugliness. There must have been beauty in the springtime when the apple trees were in blossom or in the dusk of early summer when the poplar trees sent long shadows across the river Seine, which curved about the outer edge of the village, but Yvonne could recall none of it. Only the thick brown mud that mired the roads in the fall and the bleak damp coldness of winter and the squalid farm of her parents that was like a prison, from which she could only hope to escape to another prison that would be the same.

And the blind desire for escape.

She wasn't called Yvonne then. She was Marie, the youngest of the four daughters who made her father's dour face even more bitter whenever he felt that life was treating him too harshly. Which was most of the time.

"Girls!" he would complain to his wife. "Nothing but women in the house. Just so many more mouths to feed. If you had only seen fit to give me a boy to aid me on the farm, things might have been different."

"It is as the good God wills."

"God has nothing to do with it. Perhaps some of those you lost would have been boys."

His wife bowed her head without answering. Of what good would it be to remind him that the miscarriages had been due to the unending heavy physical work that was her lot from early dawn until night. He would only point to other women who did the same labor and yet produced male children.

Marie listened silently to the wrangling arguments she knew by heart, glancing under lowered lashes from her father's sullen face with its dirty stubble of beard to her mother's patient weariness. Then she would look toward her elder sister, Germaine, whose trembling meekness beneath her father's scorn seemed like an everlasting acknowledgement of some undisclosed guilt.

The other two sisters had found local husbands and their own private slavery.

Jules grumbled about that. Just as he had once complained about their uselessness, he now complained about their leaving. "You take care of the ungrateful brats until they are old enough and big enough to be of some help, and then what happens?" he demanded. "Off they go with the first lout who is stupid enough to offer marriage!"

But it won't be that way with me, Marie would promise herself silently. She wanted to escape, too—but escape wasn't moving from the drudgery of one squalid farm to that of another. Escape was somewhere out beyond. Beyond Laverny, beyond Vernon, beyond the limits of Normandy.

It was the city.

It was Paris.

Daydreams of the city carried her through the drab monotony of the days. She was fourteen now, and a woman. She had started to develop the year before; her breasts had the round firmness of young apples and her hips were beginning to curve out from her slender waist.

The young men of the village took notice when she passed by on the road and made clumsily crude overtures. But they were only words and she could ignore them.

Only, after she had been spied upon in the river, it was different and more difficult.

That happened on a hot afternoon in the late spring. A tributary, which was scarcely wider than a brook, ran through the village and past her father's farm and joined the Seine just below the apple orchard. Poplar and willow trees shaded the spot where brook and river met and here, on warm days, Marie went alone to bathe.

On this day she had heaped her clothes on the river bank and waded out into the cooling water which rose not quite to her hips. She had brought along a thin sliver of harsh soap and she stood there covering her body with a foamy lather and then rinsing it off with cupped handfuls of water. For a time she lost herself in the pure sensual pleasure of the feeling of soap and water sliding smoothly over her flesh.

She was brought back sharply to reality by the sound of whispers and snickering laughter from the opposite bank. Quickly she turned about. Not twenty feet away, prone on the ground with only their heads visible above the tall grass, were two of the older boys of the village, Henri LeClerc and Georges Buvard.

For a long moment she stood rooted, forgetful of how fully she was exposed. Then anger and shame flared up.

"Dirty pigs! Do you have to sneak about where you have no business?"

It was Henri who answered, "The river is free. If you want to parade yourself without clothes, anyone can look."

"I'm not parading myself!"

"What do you call what you are doing now?" Words had made them bolder, and they stood up and started toward the sloping bank. "Maybe you are waiting for company. Is that it, Marie? Would you like us to teach you how to swim?"

"Perhaps she can teach us something else," Georges suggested. "I guess we have to go in the water with her to find out."

He made a gesture of unbuckling his belt.

"Filthy beasts!" Marie cried. She splashed and stumbled her way out of the water, pulled her dress over her wet body, and grabbing up her underclothes and heavy shoes raced across the fields toward home.

The story spread through the village overnight, gathering added detail as it was told and retold. After that the men stared after her more openly, their avid eyes stripping her body naked. Now they could mask their desires with a loud and heavy humor.

"It's Saturday, Marie. What time do you go to the river for your bath?"

"You should have a man along to protect you. There are wild animals waiting to pounce on tender young girls."

"At what hour does the next show go on?"

Sometimes she answered back, spitting out the curses she had heard on her father's farm since childhood. But gradually she learned that there was another, better way. She would smooth her hands over the bodice of her dress, emphasizing the outline of her breasts, and flaunt her hips as she turned away. Taunting them with the unattainable, leaving them to be tormented by their own desires....

All the while her hatred of the village and the narrow oppression of poverty increased. Yet even as she dreamed of release she faced the harsh reality of its difficulty. Some of the young men escaped from the dreary life of the small farms, but it was easier for them. They went away for their period of military service and became familiar with the larger towns and cities and when their military training was finished they stayed away, seeking opportunity elsewhere.

For the women it was another matter.

They were born and they lived and they died within the tight circumference of the village. Even marriage and the bearing of children were part of the routine pattern.

Once in a great while there was an exception.

Madame Gerlaine was one. She was the sister of Claude Brunoy, who owned the *bistro,* and she had left the village long before Marie was born. She returned once every six months or so, and her semi-annual visits were a village occasion. With her black silk dresses that fitted glovelike her full, tightly corseted figure, her high-heeled modish shoes, stylish hats, the small diamonds in her ears and larger one on her wedding finger, she was a walking emblem of success.

Rumor had it that it was her money that had bought the building and *bistro* for her brother, and that it was she who provided the money that he loaned out at exorbitant interest on farm mortgages.

When she spoke of her business in Paris she referred vaguely to a small dress shop. No one questioned her openly; respect for the power and possession of money was too deeply ingrained for that.

Behind her back, however, another story was whispered. It was common knowledge that the business that occupied Madame Gerlaine so successfully in Paris was indeed a type of shop, but one patronized exlusively by men. In short, she was the owner of a *maison de tolerance.* That in itself was nothing to be ashamed of, but whispers went further. It was said that Madame Gerlaine had, in a manner of speaking, gained her present comfortable position the hard way, by starting as an inmate in the very house she now owned. Clearly, in those years as a professional, she had been more successful than the average.

The older women of the village, discussing the matter among themselves in words coated in equal parts with malice and envy, professed not to understand it.

"I remember her well as a young girl. She was nearly seventeen when she ran away from here and certainly she was no raving beauty."

"And always acting as though butter wouldn't melt in her mouth. About those quiet ones you never can tell...."

"What men could possibly see in her to pay good money!"

"When a man is in that mood it makes no difference. *Dans le nuit tous les chats sont gris.*"

Marie had heard the stories and the whispers and the rumors as far back as she could remember. As a very small girl she had stared wide-eyed at Madame Gerlaine whenever she made one of her brief appearances, trying to turn the words she had heard into mental pictures. Now, when Madame Gerlaine made her semi-annual visit, she looked at her more thoughtfully. Here was one who had escaped—one who had achieved independence. The villagers could talk behind her back if they wanted to and say all manner of things, but to her face they were polite and respectful. And whether they were or not must have made little difference to Madame Gerlaine other than amuse her. She didn't have to spend her days in Laverny.

She had the city.

She had Paris.

It was barely a month after the incident at the river that Madame Gerlaine came back on one of her scheduled visits.

Daily, Marie found a dozen excuses to pass and repass the corner building with the *bistro* and store and living quarters overhead, hoping to catch a glimpse of the woman who was now her ideal. A few times she passed her on the road and found courage to speak.

"*Bon jour, madame.*"

"*Bon jour, ma petite.*"

But then she always became tongue-tied even though Madame Gerlaine smiled at her pleasantly. She wished she dared to say in a quick rush of words all the things that were on her mind—how she wanted to run away to Paris too and make a success of herself as Madame Gerlaine had done. And perhaps, just perhaps, Madame Gerlaine would be kind enough to advise her....

But some sixth sense besides her own hesitancy kept her silent. Instinctively she realized that it was neither the time nor the place to reveal to Madame Gerlaine that the secret of her life in Paris was no secret to Laverny.

She would have to wait.

Then she had a minor stroke of fortune. She encountered Madame Gerlaine one morning emerging from the doorway between the store and *bistro,* her arms laden down with several large packages.

Marie ran forward.

"Permit me to help you, madame."

"Thank you, little one." Madame Gerlaine gave her the customary smile, and then added an explanation. "I am taking these to the post office to mail to myself. I am leaving this afternoon and already have far too many things to carry."

Marie nodded silently, as though the difficulties of traveling with too much luggage were an old story to her.

Madame Gerlaine favored her with a closer look. "Let's see, you must be one of the daughters of Jules who has the old farm the other side of the grist mill. Am I right?"

"*Oui, madame.* I am Marie."

"A good thing for you that you weren't unfortunate enough to inherit his looks. You're quite pretty, you know. Or do all the young men in the village tell you that?"

Marie's answer was edged with bitterness. "They sometimes tell me that but they would say it anyway. Whatever words they use they are thinking of only one thing."

Madame Gerlaine eyed her sharply. Then with a half laugh she exclaimed, "*Zut!* Listen to the child, will you! And how old are you, my wise one?"

"I shall be fifteen next week."

They were nearly to the post office now and their walk had slowed down to a stop without either seeming to realize it. Madame Gerlaine stared reflectively at the girl standing silently before her, noting the wide blue eyes with their strangely violet undertones and the slim oval of the youthful face and the budding curves of the slender body that even the shapeless frock of coarse cotton couldn't quite conceal.

"Fifteen ..." she repeated slowly, but although she said the word aloud it was as though she were talking to herself. "Fifteen ..."

Then she gave herself a brusk shake in the manner of one ridding the mind of an idea that was clearly nonsense and not at all practical.

She reached out and took the packages from Marie.

"Thank you, *ma petite.* And you are too young to be too bitter or too wise. Neither will help you find romance of a good husband."

She turned to enter the post office. Marie wanted to cry after her, "Did you find either in Laverny?"

But she didn't. Instead she ran home, repeating over and over again in her mind the address she had carefully memorized from the packages she had carried for Madame Gerlaine.

It was something she didn't want to forget.

That was in early August.

It was in October that the battle with Jean Brussard occurred. That was the week when the ancient, battered still, carried in a cart drawn by two oxen, made its annual stop in Laverny. It moved from farm to farm, distilling the cider that had been pressed the year before and that had been fermenting through the long winter months, producing the raw apple brandy that when aged would be sold as Calvados.

Always the still stopped first in the clearing between Jules's farm and the old grist mill. It was the one time in the year when Jules managed to work a smile onto his face; it was pride in being the first to have his cider run through the still and a mental savoring in advance of the product. The Calvados was supposed to be for later sale in Vernon once it had aged but little ever reached the market.

Jean Brussard was the master distiller's helper. He was a local boy, but the still was owned by an uncle on his mother's side of the family who lived some twenty miles away. Working for his uncle during the fall season, moving from farm to farm and town to town, had made Jean a worldly and traveled man in the eyes of the other young men in the village. He boasted of his amorous conquests, describing in detail how each affair had come about and what had happened, and had equally detailed stories of nights spent in the more disreputable resorts of Vernon.

He had never really noticed Marie until the account of her bathing in the river before watching eyes began to be circulated.

Even then he pretended not to be interested. He dismissed the story with a shrug of his shoulders. It was something he hadn't had a hand in.

Now, however, with the still in operation on the edge of her father's farm, he found opportunity to look at her more closely. What he saw pleased him. He had heard of the way she flung tart insults back at the laughing suggestions tossed her but he knew how to handle girls of that type. You ignored their words and took them by storm and passion.

That was what they were usually waiting for....

He chose his time carefully. It was late in the afternoon when the last batch of fermented cider had been run through the still and they were waiting for the copper vat to cool so that it could be cleaned.

He saw Marie step out of the back door of the farmhouse, heading toward the rear of the barn. By now he knew the routine of her chores; she was on her way to feed the family of rabbits cooped up in a wire enclosure close by the pig pen.

He followed after her.

She spun about as his footsteps crunched on the hard earth. Her eyes narrowed as she saw the knowing grin on his face.

"What do you want?"

"Just to talk to you, Marie. I hear you like to make a show of yourself in the river. When are you going to give me a treat?"

"When you are too old for it to do you any good!"

She started to turn away with an angry toss of her head and he reached out and caught her by the arm.

"A wildcat with words, eh? Are you as quick and hot with your kisses?" He had both hands on her and was drawing her closer. "Tell me, Marie, is that what you have been waiting for? A real man to teach you how to love?"

She struggled against the strength of his arms. "Pig! Dirty son of a dirty sow! Take your filthy hands off me!"

He laughed as he tried to force her mouth to meet his own. His breath was heavy with the sour smell of raw Calvados, his unshaven chin scraped against her cheeks like harsh sandpaper. Disgust and fear sickened her, making a tight knot in her stomach.

She fought mechanically, automatically. They slipped and fell to the ground but Jean's grasp did not loosen. He was enjoying the fight. He managed a laugh as he gasped, "So this is the way you like it! But you'll be happy to lie still soon enough...."

Suddenly the cheap material of her dress gave way, ripping down the front. His hands were on her bare flesh, forcing their way over her body. She squirmed about, doubling her knees and driving a sharp elbow against his windpipe.

He moved his head back to catch his breath. "You want to fight dirty, then! Two can do the same."

All at once she remembered a story she'd once heard. He was leaning over her when she struck upward with her knee, using all the strength of primitive desperation.

He grunted in pain, clasping his hands to his hurt. In that moment of freedom Marie sprang to her feet, clutching her torn dress about her.

"*Merde!*" she spat down at him. "Specimen of filth! Now will you leave me alone?"

She turned and ran toward the house. He screamed curses after her. "Scrawny bitch! You'll pay for this. You'll pay for this a hundred times!"

Her mother looked up from her work when she stormed into the kitchen. She noticed the torn dress and the dirt and the tears of anger.

"What happened, child?"

"That dirty beast of a Jean. Behind the barn. He tried to force himself on me."

Her mother sighed heavily as she moved closer, giving Marie one of her rare gestures of affection. "That is the way with men. All of them are the same. Did he—" She paused, as if hesitating to ask a question to which she feared the answer.

Marie shook her head, "No. I got away in time."

Wearily her mother moved back to the stove. "Then you were more fortunate than most. Go change your dress before your father sees it. He will blame you for not taking better care of your things."

But that night at supper it was the mother who brought up the subject.

"You should speak to that Jean, Jules."

He looked up from his bowl of cabbage soup. He was in a good mood. He had sampled each run of the still that afternoon, and with each generous sampling had felt the burdens of poverty slipping away. "Why? What has Jean done?"

"He tried to take Marie by force this afternoon."

Jules turned his glance toward his youngest daughter. She was sitting with downcast eyes, toying with the food in front of her as though her mind were elsewhere. But when she felt her father's gaze on her she raised her head and stared back at him.

Jules laughed. "Jean is a good boy. A girl could find a worse husband."

"He said nothing about marriage," Marie flared angrily. "He wanted only one thing."

Again her father laughed. "So? And how do you think most girls snare their husbands?" He turned a bitter look at his wife. "Ask your mother. She could teach you a trick or two about that!"

"Jules!" her mother cried out.

"Jules!" he mocked. He lurched up from the table. "Believe me, it is not the girls who need protection from such as Jean. It is the men who get trapped. Trapped for all their lives!"

Marie waited until all the household was asleep. As she slipped out of bed and started to dress she could hear the heavy breathing of her sister Germaine in the other bed. From across the hall came the sound of her father's drunken snoring—a sound that for the first time in her life she welcomed.

She dressed quickly and carefully. She had few things to carry with her, no more than a small bundle of underclothes and her Sunday dress.

She new where the crockery jar was hidden in the kitchen; the place where her mother hoarded the few francs she was able to keep from Jules' grasping fingers. She took no more than she thought would be necessary.

Outside there was a moon but it was partially obscured by scudding clouds. It was better that way, in the darkness there was less danger of being seen.

It was a dozen long miles to Vernon and the railroad station but that made no matter either. She had things to think about along the way and dreams to keep her company. She knew what she wanted and where she was going.

It was to Paris.

To the house of Madame Gerlaine.

CHAPTER THREE

THE ADDRESS OF Madame Gerlaine was in a narrow side street just off the rue Blondel.

It was midmorning when at last Marie found her way there, and she stood for a long moment staring at the shuttered windows. There was a queer tremor in her heart, a fluttery feeling that was a mixture of hesitancy and something akin to fear. For a breathless space of time she was tempted to turn away, until she remembered forlornly that now she had nowhere else to go.

This was where her plans and her dreams of escape had led her.

This was the end of one road and the beginning of another.

Resolutely she reached for the heavy brass knocker on the door.

She had to knock repeatedly and a new fear assailed her that possibly she had been wrong in her memory of the address. Then at last there was the sound of heavy locks being turned and the door swung open a few inches, enough to permit the dour, wrinkled face of a cleaning woman to peer out.

"What is it at this hour? Can't you see the place isn't open yet?"

"I wish only to speak to Madame Gerlaine."

"Impossible! She is still asleep." The servant started to close the door. "Return some time in the afternoon. Perhaps she can see you then."

"But I can't return in the afternoon," Marie insisted stubbornly. "I am from Laverny, madame's home town. She wouldn't like it if you forced me to remain waiting in the streets."

The closing door became motionless. Beady, suspicious eyes swept over Marie, appraising what they saw with a wary shrewdness.

"From Laverny, you say?"

"That is correct." Marie shifted her small bundle of belongings from one arm to the other. She added a statement that she hoped in time would come true. "I am an old friend of madame's and her family."

The answer to that was a noncommittal grunt. Nevertheless the door opened at bit wider. At the same time the woman grumbled, "Then perhaps you had better come in, although the madame certainly said nothing about expecting a visitor. You can wait in the kitchen and when she awakens I will tell her that you are here. What name shall I say?"

"Marie. Marie Courcel, the daughter of old Jules who lives by the grist mill."

As Marie slipped into the hallway she glanced about surreptitiously. She wasn't sure in her mind what she had thought to find, but certainly it wasn't this air of almost drab respectability. She wondered nervously if the whispers and rumors in Laverny as to Madame Gerlaine's profession had been no more than that—idle, malicious gossip without foundation.

She was vaguely reassured when she entered the kitchen, Here at least were evidences of some sort of festivity. There was a profusion of empty wine and champagne bottles, stacked in one corner. The sink was filled with dirty glasses. As the cleaning woman started to work on them with a wheezy grumble which seemed to be habitual, Marie offered tentatively, "Perhaps I could help you while I am waiting for madame."

The wheezy grumble stopped. "As you wish. It's seldom that anybody offers to help old Louise these days. When I was younger it was different—then there were men always offering to help." She broke off and gave a little cackle of obscene reminiscence. "But the help had nothing to do with washing dishes, of that you may be sure."

Marie looked at her quickly, then away. Was it possible that this embittered drudge had once been young and attractive, with men eager to buy her favors? Had she once been an inmate of such a house as this and was this the inevitable fate of all such women, with nothing left but fading memories?

For a moment there was an emptiness within her, an uneasy, questioning doubt. And then she remembered Madame Gerlaine and her obvious success and security. Without realizing it she gave her head a toss and her young lips set in a thin line of determination.

It was Madame Gerlaine she would keep always in mind as an inspiration. Not old Louise, the drudge....

It was a full two hours later before Madame Gerlaine came downstairs. She appeared suddenly in the kitchen doorway, demanding sharply what had happened to delay her coffee. A nightcap still covered her jet-black hair and she clutched a gray flannel bathrobe about her middle. It was clear that as yet she had not forced her bulging flesh into the rigid prison of a corset.

It was a moment before she noticed Marie sitting quietly in a corner and then she questioned impatiently, "Who is this girl, Louise? What is she doing here?"

It was Marie herself who answered.

"Don't you remember me, Madame Gerlaine? I am Jules's daughter, Marie. From Laverny."

Madame Gerlaine frowned.

"And how did you find your way here?"

"I remembered your address from the time I helped you carry some packages to the post office. That was when you were in Laverny in the spring."

"So? But why should my address interest you?"

Marie hesitated, glancing swiftly in the direction of old Louise and then back at Madame Gerlaine. Then she lowered her eyes and said softly, "For reasons. Reasons only you could understand."

Madame Gerlaine gave her another penetrating look.

"You mean you're in trouble? *Enceinte?*"

Marie felt herself blushing as she shook her head. "No. It's nothing like that. I've never—I'm still—" She broke off in faint confusion, glancing again at the attentively listening Louise.

The puzzled, slightly annoyed frown remained on Madame Gerlaine's face as she shrugged and suggested without enthusiasm, "Bring your coffee up to my room where we can talk in private. But I still don't understand why you should seek me out...."

Ten minutes later when Marie had finished her halting story the annoyance was replaced by something like shocked amazement.

"Ridiculous!" Madame Gerlaine exclaimed. *"Incroyable!* Why, you're only fifteen—a mere child. And still a virgin!"

"It is not the fault of the men of Laverny that I am," Marie said bluntly. "And as for being fifteen—do I look no more than that?"

"That has nothing to do with it. I refuse to be responsible for introducing you to such a life. Think what the people of Laverny would say once they learned of the truth."

"But the people of Laverny will never know," Marie persisted. "Whatever happens, I shall never return there nor write to anyone there. And if you do not care to help me I will find another house or go on the streets."

Madame Gerlaine set her coffee cup down with an impatient gesture. "You're a stubborn little wench, aren't you?" Then when Marie only stared back at her without answering she went on, "I half believe you mean what you say. But it isn't as easy as you might think for a girl on the streets—even a fresh and pretty young thing like yourself. There are the police on every corner and the *flics* in plain clothes and the pimps lurking everywhere, all waiting to take a part of your earnings. Then there is the matter of your yellow ticket which at your age might not be so easy to procure." She paused and gave a sigh heavy with reminiscence of things long past. "No, it isn't by any means an easy life."

"I don't expect an easy life. I want only to be independent as you are, madame. I don't want to spend all my years slaving for one man, like the women at home."

For a long moment Madame Gerlaine stared at her, then gave an odd laugh. "So instead of serving one man you prefer to serve a multitude. But perhaps at that you have the right idea, although the good God alone knows how you came by it. And certainly you have determination." She closed her eyes as if trying to see somewhere in her mind an answer to the problem. Finally she murmured in a voice so low that it was almost as though she were talking to herself, "I shouldn't do it, I know. It is all wrong. Only I keep remembering myself when I was your age and I remember Laverny only too well. And if I do not help you God alone knows where you will end up...."

Her words trailed off and she gave another weary sigh as she spread her hands out in a sign of resignation.

Wisely, Marie remained silent.

Her introduction into an active participation in the life of the establishment was not immediate.

Madame Gerlaine, once she had overcome her early scruples, reverted to type. She became shrewdly calculating, appraising

Marie with the practiced eye of one long experienced in catering to the whims and caprices of masculine desire.

"There is no point in rushing matters," she announced. "At the moment you have something very special and there are men who pay tidy sums to be the first. A foolishness and a waste of good money, if you ask me, but that is the way of things. And later it would be stupid to use you for the ordinary client. You have youth, and that is always worth more. Providing, naturally, that you have a flair for the profession."

"I can learn," Marie promised.

Madame Gerlaine smiled slightly. "Some things, my child, are a matter of feeling and not of practice. But we shall see what we shall see."

Meantime, Marie had met the other inmates of the house. There were six in all. They trailed down to dinner in the late afternoon, clustering about a table in an alcove off the kitchen. Most were in soiled dressing gowns that had once been cheaply garish. Some were without makeup, their cheeks puffy and their eyes still swollen with sleep. At the beginning of the meal there was little conversation, not until after the hot soup and a glass of *vin ordinaire* did the girls speak in more than monosyllables.

The half dozen *poules* represented a variety of types that later Marie learned was by no means accidental. There was Annette, a dark-skinned girl from the shores of the Mediterranean. Another brunette, who called herself Gigi, was from Avignon, while another even darker haired girl was clearly Russian. There was a blonde, Marcelle, and a redhead, Lizette. Both were Paris born and bred and as a result felt and acted slightly superior to the other girls who hailed from less sophisticated spots.

Finally there was Berta, La Vache. Berta was from Alsace-Lorraine, of mixed French-German parentage. Her nickname was singularly appropriate and not alone because of the slightly bovine, expressionless placidity of her chubby features. Even in the practice of her profession she maintained the same cowlike acceptance toward whatever happened, apparently untouched and unmoved by the quick succession of men who momentarily possessed her.

She didn't even appear to mind being called The Cow, or if she did she gave no sign of it. She spoke little, and then usually only in answer to direct questions. When she wasn't at work or on display with the other girls in the front parlor, she was busy with sewing or embroidery, frowning intently over the small, painstaking stitches.

The other girls taunted her.

"La Vache is working on her hope chest. Who is the lucky man going to be, Berta?"

"Do you think she'll tell *us*? But I heard it was a baron, no less. He fell in love with her mind."

"Will you keep on working here to support him, Berta?"

For answer Berta only smiled.

Yet it was clear that she was one of Madame Gerlaine's favorites. There was a reason, which the madame explained to Marie. "Berta is a good girl. True, she is a peasant and without chic and can never hope to rise above a certain level in this profession. I suspect, too, that she is without emotions, and that is all the better. These other girls who allow themselves to become excited burn themselves out too quickly. In this life it is wise to learn to control one's feelings."

Marie listened and watched and stored each stray bit of information away in her mind. Her first night in the house Madame Gerlaine had ordered her to remain in the room that had been assigned her.

"There is time enough for you to begin. But first there are other important things to do. Tomorrow we will see about getting the proper attire for you. The money I will advance, to come out of your future earnings."

It was not until two nights later that Marie was initiated into her chosen career. Then it was with an elderly roué whose stimulation was more mental than physical. Marie suffered his time-tested caresses with more curiosity than fear. At times her body responded without conscious volition to new sensations she wasn't quite certain she enjoyed, but at the same time her mind remained resolutely objective.

It was as though she were two persons; the one a young girl who was almost a stranger to her, whose body was being subjected to hitherto little-imagined rites, the other her real self.

At the same time she was dimly aware of a vague feeling of frustration. She had experienced neither the pain nor the pleasure she had been led by hearsay to expect.

Her first six months in the establishment passed quickly. Bit by bit she became accustomed to the routine, to the turning of day into night, just as she became accustomed to the variety of customers who requested her services. Mostly, as a result of Madame Gerlaine's subtle suggestions, they were older men.

"With you, *ma petite,* they have for a little while the illusion of youth." She paused and permitted herself one of her rare laughs as she rubbed her thumb and forefinger together. "And illusions are always an expensive luxury, although most never discover it until too late. Which is possibly just as well for those of us whose business is pretense...."

Marie nodded, thinking of the little bundle of carefully horded franc notes that was increasing each week. At least there was no illusion about money—it was something firm and tangible and reassuring. It spelled independence sometime in the future. And thinking of that future, and of the moment, she was reasonably content.

She felt she was doing well. Laverny seemed no more than part of a faintly remembered dream.

Consequently, she was somewhat surprised when Madame Gerlaine summoned her to her room one noon and announced bluntly, "The time has come to talk seriously about your work."

Marie stared at her blankly. "My work? But I thought—You mean, there have been complaints?"

Madame made one of her typically impatient gestures. "To the contrary. You have done very well for a beginner. You have even developed your own clientele, which is always a mark of progress in this profession."

"Then I don't understand—"

"Naturally. I take it that at the moment you are quite satisfied with everything as it is?"

"But of course. You have been very kind, madame."

Madame Gerlaine dismissed the idea of kindness with a brusk wave of one hand. "For the first day only I was kind. After that it was a matter of business. And it is of business I now wish to speak." She paused, studying Marie appraisingly for a long moment. "I have watched you carefully in the months you have been here. I felt a certain sense of responsibility, as you may well understand. And my early judgment wasn't wrong—it is clear that you have a talent for attracting and pleasing men of a certain type."

"Thank you, madame."

Madame grunted. "Don't be too quick with your thanks until you hear the rest. It is true enough that you have a flair for love-making, but when it comes to other qualities it is another matter. Outside of the bedroom you are still what you are—a country girl with no chic, no *savoir-faire*. You even talk like a Normandy peasant."

Marie's first reaction was one of wounded anger. Then she said sullenly, "I wasn't aware that men came here to listen to conversation."

"Nor do they," Madame Gerlaine admitted. "But that is another matter again. And there is no need of your acting hurt or upset for I am talking for your own good. This isn't the only establishment of its kind in Paris. I pride myself on running a respectable, middle-class place for a respectable, middle-class clientele. But it has its limitations, as I am only too well aware. You could remain here indefinitely and never advance beyond a certain point."

Marie was still puzzled and confused. She said hesitantly, "It sounds as though you were trying to discourage me or get rid of me or something of the sort. Is that it, madame?"

"I am only trying to give you the benefit of experience. Without education you are only a body that in time will age and lose its appeal. You have a peasant's respect for money so it is unlikely that you will end up in the manner of old Lucille. But neither will you have taken full advantage of the opportunities that could be yours."

"But what opportunities, madame?"

"To make the most of yourself, for one thing. To become an individual of importance instead of just one more of the thousands of pretty little creatures who sell their bodies at the market price. No profession is worth being in unless you have ambitions to rise to the top."

"But you—"

Madame Gerlaine cut her short. "I am not the one under discussion. Besides, I was born to be a business woman, not a *fille de joie*. I merely made the most of such capabilities as I possessed. Now I am in hopes that you will see the wisdom of doing the same."

That was when she began describing a world that up to then Marie had not realized existed. It was a luxurious world, peopled in the main by men of wealth and women of exceptional charm. "Not mere beauty, which is common enough," Madame insisted, "but charm. A whim of nature gives one a pretty face and figure, but charm is something that must be learned. True, in the end these women are no more than prostitutes, but they are prostitutes de luxe. It is even possible that in the actual practice of their trade they are no more expert than any of the girls here, yet in place of earning a few hundred francs a night they know nothing smaller than a thousand-franc note. The difference is due to the fact that they have properly educated themselves for their profession."

And I am without that education, Marie thought with a tinge of bitterness. Certainly madame had made that clear enough. But it was less clear what was expected of her now.

The answer was quickly forthcoming.

"Educating themselves," Madame Gerlaine repeated, "as I now propose that you educate yourself. With my assistance, naturally. And providing, at the same time, that you have sufficient ambition...."

For Marie, that was the beginning of another chapter in her life.

Madame Gerlaine's ideas on education were unorthodox but, nevertheless, strict. She was satisfied only with the best of teachers, even though she bargained shrewdly when it came to a matter of payment. Thus it was a middle-aged professor from the Sorbonne, a fortnightly visitor to the establishment, who was engaged to tutor Marie in the proper use of her own language. But no money was involved—it was, in a manner of speaking, an exchange of professional services. The same sort of an arrangement was made with an English remittance man, also a regular habitué of the *maison,* to introduce Marie into the complexities of his native tongue.

That was on the academic side. But there were other subjects that Madame Gerlaine insisted had an equal importance, lessons that could not be learned from a book but only by experience. Hence it was a buyer for a small wholesale wine house who initiated Marie into the art of judging and savoring good wines and a tobacco importer who taught her how to pass judgement on a Havana cigar by studying the age and texture or the leaf as well as by sniffing the aroma.

Once, through one of her at times mysterious connections, Madame Gerlaine found temporary employment for Marie as a stock girl in the show rooms of one of the leading *couturiers.*

"If you are alert and keep your eyes open you need only remain there a few weeks," she advised. "It is an opportunity for you to observe how women of fashion dress and comport themselves."

Again at odd intervals, but usually on a Monday or Tuesday when business was light, madame would leave the establishment in charge of Berta, La Vache, and take Marie on an outing. It might be to the races at Long-champs, if it were the season, or to Rumplemeyer's or the Ritz for tea. Or, at a later hour, dinner at Maxim's or Prunier's or Le Boef sur la Toit. Wherever it might be, Madame Gerlaine's interest was always the same—that of pointing out to Marie various famous figures of the Parisian demimonde. Madame was remarkably well versed in their individual biographies; this one had started her career as a nude waitress in a café-brothel on the rue Blondel, another had risen from the vice-slums of the rue du Lappe, a third had been a model passing from the bed of one penniless artist to that of another before she awakened to the fact that she was working at two professions and profiting from neither.

"You can see for yourself how well they have done. It is because they have pride in their craft, because they were not content to merely rest on their *derrières* staring at the ceiling. Ambition is what counts, my little one."

Marie nodded and spoke what had been in her mind for a long time.

"You are very kind to go to so much trouble...."

"It is not kindness at all!" Madame Gerlaine said sharply. "Neither my heart nor my head have gone that soft. Rest assured that if you are a success and I am able to enter you into the house I have in mind I shall lose nothing by it. I shall have my proper commission, never fear!"

It was inevitable that Marie's activities would attract comment from the other girls in the house. They were jealous of the fact that she was clearly Mme Gerlaine's protégée and only on call for a certain type of client. When old Lucille reported that both were from the same village in Normandy it was whispered that Marie was actually the madame's daughter. The madame was notoriously tight-fisted, watching every *sou*, and how else could one explain such things as the teachers and clothes and the outings?

Yet for the most part they contented themselves with barbed remarks tossed with apparent casualness into the air.

"I hear that soon there will be a new type of examination before one may enter a house of this sort. Unless you can speak like an aristocratic *jeune fille* you will be out on the street."

"Will they mark your grades on your yellow ticket along with your health report?"

"And one must always be dressed in the latest *mode*...."

"*Quelle blague!* With my customers it is what I don't wear that counts."

Only Berta, La Vache, did not join in the thinly veiled taunts. Possibly because she, herself, had been the victim of so many—possibly because she dimly understood the purpose behind Marie's unusual program. In the early afternoons she would bring her sewing into Marie's room and sit quietly while the latter frowned in concentration over her lessons for the week.

Once she said shyly, "You should pay no attention to what the other girls say. It is well to have a goal in such a life as this. Otherwise it would be just a stupidity...."

Marie glanced up at her in faint surprise. "And you have a goal, Berta?"

"But naturally. In a few more months I will have saved enough for a respectable *dot,* sufficient to purchase a small farm."

"And the young man you intend to marry. Have you picked him out?"

La Vache nodded, her eyes intent on the sewing in her lap. "It has been understood for a long time. He is a boy in my home village." She hesitated, then added slowly, "He is serious and a hard worker. He will make a good husband."

Mischievously Marie asked, "And he is a good lover, as well?"

Bera flushed and said in a shocked tone, "But, how should I know such a thing? We are not married as yet—only betrothed."

"Then he doesn't know the profession you are following here?"

"But certainly he knows. How else would I explain the money I am saving? But he realizes that this is merely a matter of business. It does not give him the right to take liberties." She bent over her sewing again and finished almost primly, "After all, if one is too free with a man before marriage he is apt to take too much for granted. And it is well for a wife to always have respect in her own home."

It was a remark that Marie was to remember a long time later.

Meanwhile her education continued. The peasant accent and peasant phrases of the Normandy countryside were replaced with the softer, smoother speech of the Parisian upper class. She had learned how to walk and to dress with the proper air; she was no longer timid and ill at ease when madame took her to a smart restaurant nor mystified by a lengthy gourmet's menu. She could order a dinner with judgment and select the proper wines for each course.

By then she had grown several inches and the early promise of her youthful figure had been fulfilled. She was slender and long-legged, with firm, upright breasts and hips that swelled out from a narrow waist. The soft waves of her carefully tended hair were now the shimmering blue-black color of coal, making the deep blue of her eyes seem more nearly violet than ever.

Men began to notice her on the streets and to stare openly in the smart cafés. Each time Madame Gerlaine bristled with a vicarious pride.

"You see, *ma petite?* Already the lessons you have learned are bearing fruit."

"What fruit?" Marie demanded with a doubtful smile. "Just having men ogle me doesn't increase my savings any."

"Patience," Madame Gerlaine advised. "Everything in its time. Even now I am discussing your future with an acquaintance of mine who has a most exclusive place on the rue Litre. She wishes to see you in person, and if you comport yourself correctly—" Madame paused and spread out her hands. "If you are fortunate enough to be accepted you will be a very lucky girl. Far luckier than I was at your age, I may tell you!"

That was how, just two months shy of her eighteenth birthday, Marie first entered the discreetly famous establishment presided over by Madame Romain.

For a moment, standing before the massive outer doors wait-ing for the butler to answer her ring and fetch her luggage from the cab, she remembered that other day that now seemed so long ago, when she had stood hesitantly before the door of the house just off the rue Blondel, frightened and hesitant and nervous. Half tempted to turn and flee, only to realize that she had no other destination.

Now all that was behind her. It was gone with her awkward-ness and her ignorance and her peasant manners. The period of her apprenticeship was over.

Even the name she had brought with her from Laverny was cast aside.

She was no longer Marie.

Now she was Yvonne.

Yvonne of the Maison d'Or.

CHAPTER FOUR

S HE FINISHED SPEAKING and fell silent for a long moment. Then she arose and, crossing to the window, drew back the heavy drapes and flung wide the night shutters. Outside, the night had given way to the misty gray of a Paris dawn.

At last she turned back to face the room, a faint smile curving her lips. "So you see, my friend, there is no tragedy to my being where you find me. I was not seduced and then betrayed by some heartless lover, as the storybooks and the movies have you believe always happens. Rather I am, as the good Madame Gerlaine so often points out, a very fortunate girl."

Boardman stared at her in perplexity, not quite certain what to say. His mind was a muddle of contradictory thoughts. The old-fashioned euphemisms of his ancestors were still a subconscious part of his vocabulary. There were polite synonyms for whores—a "fallen woman" was one who had been pushed involuntarily into a life of harlotry by adverse forces, while a woman of "easy virtue" was one too lazy to make an honest living.

That one could regard such a life as a profession, and actually take pride in the accomplishment, was a new and startling thought.

He was aware that Yvonne was speaking again.

"You are, perhaps, a little disappointed that my story was not more dramatic?"

He shook his head. "To me it sounded more than dramatic." Looking up at her standing before him in the center of the room, he tried to picture in his mind the untutored, ill-dressed country girl she had described. It was impossible. "More than dramatic," he repeated. "It is almost incredible. I can't believe that you were ever different than you are now."

"Thank you, m'sieu. That would mean that I have learned my lessons well." She moved over to the ice bucket, twirling a champagne bottle idly with slender fingertips. "Another glass of wine? Or perhaps at this hour you would prefer coffee?"

Boardman glanced at his watch and for the first time realized the hour. "It is both too late and too early," he said, as he got to his feet. "And I have kept you up all the night."

"There is always the day to sleep in. Besides, I was talking about myself and every woman enjoys that at times."

To his own surprise, Boardman found himself suggesting, "And if I come back again?"

"That is for you to say, m'sieu."

He hesitated, uncertain as to the next move, then started to withdraw his wallet from an inner pocket. She stopped him with a little gesture.

"Such matters are arranged below with Madame Romain."

"But, look here," Boardman insisted, finding himself fumbling for words. "I mean I've taken up so much of your time. Surely a present of some sort—"

Again she stopped him.

"This was not that kind of evening, *mon ami,*" she reminded him softly. "It would rather spoil things to receive anything in return."

"Another time then, perhaps...."

"Perhaps." She smiled as she held out her hand. *"A bientôt,* my friend. Until another time."

"Soon, I hope," Boardman found himself saying. "Very soon."

A damned strange girl, he told himself in the taxi headed toward the Crillon. A damned remarkable girl, if you came down to it.

And damned honest, at the same time.

Boardman's appointment with Helen Avery and her mother for luncheon was, as usual, at the Ritz. And, as was also usual, they were a half hour late.

He stopped in the men's bar for a quick drink, elbowing his way through the throng that lined the bar three deep. He heard his name called and, turning about, saw that it was Bill Chase, manager of the Paris branch of the First National Trust, waving to him from a table against the far wall. Glass in hand, Boardman made his way across the room.

"How's the market this morning, Bill?"

"The same as ever. Going up, up, up with no ceiling in sight. But the more important question is, how the hell are you?"

Boardman frowned down at him over the edge of his highball glass.

"The same as ever. Why should I be any different?"

Chase raised a quizzical eyebrow. "Well, all I know is that I helped pour Larry Brewster and Stover on the boat train this morning. And *they* looked a little the worse for wear. The way they tell the story, you were with them up to a certain point and then evaporated into thin air. They were a bit confused as to just when and how."

"Confused is the right word," Boardman told him smoothly. "I don't wonder that they couldn't remember leaving me. I'm only surprised that they recalled that they were sailing today."

He declined Chase's invitation to another drink and left the bar in search of Helen and her mother. It was a good thing Brewster and Stover had left Paris, he told himself. Given one too many, they both talked too damned much.

Although, when you came down to it, he had nothing to feel guilty about himself.

He started slowly along Peacock Alley toward the entrance facing the Place Vendome, his way hampered every few feet by little groups of obvious tourists. Men were in the minority—it seemed to Boardman that the entire Ritz, with the exception of the men's bar, had been taken over by some girls' finishing school that had suddenly got out of hand. That was the year that fashion dictated knee-length, sheathlike dresses and flat figures; with their bobbed hair and bangs and plucked eyebrows, their high-pitched chatter and thin, excited squeals, they seemed as alike as two peas in a pod.

No wonder the French have such a distorted idea of Americans, he thought irritably, and in the same moment found himself thinking of the contrasting quietness and femininity of the girl he had left only a few hours before.

It was a full half hour past the appointed time when Helen and Mrs. Avery appeared. Helen, too, was a carbon copy of the current mode. She was taller than average and thus seemed thinner than she actually was, an illusion heightened by her quick, nervous mannerisms. Her skin was usually so deeply tanned that she needed little makeup but she affected a vivid lip rouge that brought out the reddish tones in her brown hair, clipped in what was then known as a wind-blown bob.

Mrs. Avery, on the other hand, was short and inclined toward plumpness. Although it was now more than two years since her husband had passed on, she wore her widowhood like an almost visible cloak. She dressed in delicate pastel colors; she smiled constantly but it was always a patient, wistful smile. She had baby-blue eyes into which one had to look more than once to discover that they held neither softness nor warmth.

It was Helen who spotted Boardman first, standing just inside the entrance.

"Darling! Did we keep you waiting long? But it was mother's fault—she was on the telephone talking simply for hours!"

Mrs. Avery flicked a quick look at her daughter, then smiled up at Boardman. "But you'll forgive me, won't you?"

"Of course. You weren't really late at all. In Paris no one is expected to be on time."

Helen gave his arm a squeeze. "You're so understanding, Winnie. Most men would raise a fuss if they were kept waiting so long. But you never do." She was sending little darting glances about as she talked, and now she added, "Where did all these people come from? We'll never get a table in all this crush. That's the trouble with Paris in the summer—too many tourists!"

Boardman found himself tempted to remind her that they were tourists themselves. Instead he merely said, "Don't worry about a table. I've already reserved one."

"Darling! I keep forgetting you're so practical. You always think of everything, don't you?"

"Not always."

Luncheon developed into the disrupted meal it usually was at the Ritz. Mrs. Avery spent the greater part of the time bowing to or acknowledging greetings of friends. People continually paused at the table; Boardman had to rise so often that he felt like a jumping-jack. Then, during a temporary lull from such interruptions, Helen became facetiously curious about the night before.

"How did you boys make out on the town last night?"

Boardman shrugged. "Just the usual thing. The *Folies* and then a round of the night clubs. One is pretty much like another, though."

"And afterward?"

"Home to bed," Boardman said, pretending not to understand.

Helen smiled knowingly. "I imagine. But not alone, of course."

"Helen!" Mrs. Avery exclaimed with mechanical disapproval. "Really, my dear ..."

"But, mother! I'm simply being frank. I can't feature three single men out on a fling managing to withstand temptation so firmly. Not with all Paris swarming with beautiful *cocottes*. If I were a man—"

"Helen!" her mother cut in again. "Such subjects aren't to be joked about."

Boardman tried to bring the matter to a close. He said with careful casualness, "I can't answer for Brewster or Stover, I'm afraid. We parted company shortly after midnight. I had a headache and wasn't in a mood for making a night of it."

That at least was essentially the truth, he told himself. They *had* separated sometime after midnight. He *hadn't* felt in the mood for dissipation. His words presented the skeleton of fact without the flesh of reality.

Before Helen could take up the probe again he went on, "How about this afternoon? We haven't made any plans, have we? I thought we might take in the races and then drive over to St. Cloud for an early dinner. I understand there's a very decent restaurant there."

Helen gave a small sigh of regret. "But darling! Why didn't you suggest it before? I have an appointment for a fitting at Patou's this afternoon that I can't possibly miss."

Boardman started to nod. Then a memory struck him. "But I thought it was yesterday you went to Patou's. When I called your hotel in the afternoon your mother said—"

She cut in before he could finish. "Mother always gets every-thing wrong. I went to Henri's to see about some hats." She turned to Mrs. Avery and said almost sharply, "Don't you remember, mother? I said distinctly that I was going to Henri's yesterday because today I had this other appointment with Patou."

There was a moment's silence, and then Mrs. Avery said tonelessly, "You must be right, Helen. I imagine I wasn't listening too clearly."

Boardman was watching her hands as she spoke, watch-ing thin fingers nervously crumbling a crust of bread. He was vaguely conscious of a tension in the air.

He found himself wondering silently, what the hell goes on, anyway?

CHAPTER FIVE

M ORE THAN ONCE during the past weeks Boardman had caught himself wondering exactly how his engagement to Helen Avery had come about. To a great extent, he supposed, it was because he had always known her. They had been born and reared in the same Connecticut town—a town noted for its per capita wealth and large estates. They belonged to the same clubs, moved in the same exclusive circles, and had a similarity of interests.

Boardman was essentially an outdoor man. Cocktail parties and club dances bored him, as did the fad of contract bridge, which was beginning to sweep the country. And he was equally unresponsive to the new crop of debutantes that had suddenly appeared on the social horizon. Their loud, brash manners alarmed him; he was never quite certain they knew the full implications of half they were saying. They drank too much and talked too much and were always on the quest for synthetic excitement.

Helen Avery was an exception to the formula. She, too, was fond of sports. She played a better than average game of golf and tennis, was a good hand at sailing, and an accomplished horsewoman.

Boardman felt at ease with her.

Gradually he saw more and more of her, and became automatically paired off with her at dinner parties and club dances. He increased his attentions when her father passed away, remembering his own feeling of sudden loss when his own father had been lost in the Titanic disaster, a decade before.

There was a generally prevalent rumor that old John Avery had left an estate considerably smaller than might have been expected, that it had been business reverses that had brought on the heart attack that had led to his death. But if this were true, Mrs. Avery gave no outward indication of the fact. After a brief period of mourning she became as socially active as ever. She kept up expensive club memberships, gave her usual quota of teas and dinner parties, dressed her daughter in the latest fashions.

Boardman found himself a more constant visitor at the Avery home. By now he had become an active partner in his father's old firm in Wall Street, and at intervals Mrs. Avery would call him on the telephone.

"I wonder if I could trouble you for some advice, Winthrop. It's about some changes in my investments that the bank recommends, and I know so little about such things."

"Of course, Mrs. Avery."

"Then perhaps you could stop in for a moment for cocktails on your way home. Or for dinner, if you haven't a previous engagement."

It was only natural that Helen should usually be there, too.

By then Boardman was twenty-five and had begun thinking seriously of marriage. He didn't greatly care for a bachelor's freedom; his mother was only rarely in Old Haven, preferring Bar Harbor in the summer and Florida or the Italian Riviera in the winter months. The big house was lonely, and Boardman discovered himself increasingly envying friends of his age who already had their own homes and families. That was the only way for a man to live.

Helen Avery seemed the logical choice.

That had been barely two months ago. Almost immediately following the announcement of the engagement Helen and her mother had announced plans for a European trip.

"But, look here!" Boardman had half protested. "You didn't say anything about going to Europe before. I thought we'd have fun together this summer and go to Europe on our honeymoon."

"And we will, too, darling," Helen assured him brightly. "Only now mother and I have to run over to Paris to pick out my trousseau. You men never understand about such things."

There were a great many things he didn't understand, Boardman decided in the period that followed. The Avery's Paris jaunt had prolonged itself far beyond the allotted three weeks; in her sketchy, hastily scrawled letters Helen was vague as to the exact date of their return. The excuses varied—the Paris *couturiers* were either incredibly slow or incredibly rushed; it was impossible to get anything done in a minute, as at home; she was having an especially divine wedding gown fashioned by Maurice, who was very temperamental and refused to be hurried, and naturally she couldn't leave before it was finished. But next week, surely....

The lack of any organized, concrete schedule began to annoy Boardman. Both in his business affairs in Wall Street and in his private life he was accustomed to spend considerable time making up his mind over a project, but once he had come to a definite decision he was in the habit of going ahead without further delay.

He didn't like dawdling and procrastination.

Now he had sold himself on the comfortable picture of a happy, conventional marriage. That meant an attentive, dutiful, and charming wife and in due time a pair of equally dutiful and charming children. And having the picture so firmly placed in his mind he was disturbed to discover that it couldn't become reality overnight.

At the same time he began to wonder if this casualness of Helen's in the matter of making a plan and sticking to it would carry over into their marriage.

He hoped not.

In the end he had decided on a quick trip to Paris to find out at first hand what was causing the delay. But to date, he was forced to admit, he hadn't accomplished much. Helen seemed caught up in a mysterious web of engagements and conflicting engagements, appointments that she always explained with a quick, hectic rush of words which in the end sometimes explained nothing. And Mrs. Avery, behind her plaintive wistfulness, seemed oddly tense and nervous.

It wasn't the way things ought to go, Boardman told himself.

It wasn't the way at all.

CHAPTER SIX

T WICE DURING THE week that followed Boardman returned to the house on the rue Litre. Each time it was on the spur of the moment, the result of being left at loose ends for the late evening due to a sudden headache developed by Helen Avery.

"Do you mind frightfully, Winthrop, if we call it a night? My head is simply splitting."

No, he had told her, under the circumstances, he didn't mind. But he had been faintly puzzled and disturbed. Helen had always made almost a fetish out of her exuberant good health, she was impatient with those of her sex who pampered themselves for minor illnesses. "It's all in the mind," she used to say. "Most people just think themselves into being sick."

But now, apparently, her mind had changed.

Boardman wasn't quite certain what it was, on those evenings that Helen begged off from whatever plans they had tentatively made, that drew him back to Yvonne. Of only one thing he was sure—it wasn't for the obvious reason. There was no questioning Yvonne's sexual magnetism, of that Boardman had been sharply aware since the first time he set eyes on her. But the mood set that first night when he had been somewhat reluctantly introduced to the house by Larry Brewster was difficult to shake off; he had the strange feeling that he would be taking advantage of a friendship if he indicated to Yvonne that he expected her to fulfill her professional obligations to him.

True, she was a whore and he was paying for her services and her time. But using her as an outlet for mechanical passion would break the spell. Then their relationship, which as yet Boardman had not stopped to analyze, would inevitably change.

He would be just one more client.

As it was he was able to relax in Yvonne's presence, free from any nagging sense of guilt. He was constantly intrigued by her deft sense of hospitality; she made him feel, in an odd way, at home.

At the same time he had the usual outsider's curiosity as to her life and her personal reactions to it. The idea that she had to submit to passion, whether she felt like it or not, still seemed to him a degrading form of slavery.

Once he managed to put his thoughts into clumsy words and Yvonne answered him with a mocking smile, saying, "And what is marriage, my friend? Only a few women marry for love alone. The others are usually seeking more worldly things—a home and security and a future without work or worry. In return they submit not only their bodies but their independence."

"But just to one man," Boardman protested.

She raised a questioning eyebrow. "So? Then is it a matter of numbers and not of morals? Yet at any given moment the end result is the same—a woman is sleeping with a man, not through desire, but because she has sold herself."

Boardman had no quick answer. He found himself thinking of a good many of his friends who were caught up in loveless marriages. He was remembering the fragments of casual conversation heard at country clubs and dinner parties, with some wife loudly proclaiming, "John would like half a dozen children at least running about the house. But I told him flatly from the start that two were enough. No more for me, thank you. I didn't marry to turn myself into a breeding mare!" Bargains made and sometimes kept. Value for value received. Maybe that was the reason some races still had recourse to marriage brokers. If it was just a business proposition, why not?

He was jostled back to the present to find Yvonne refilling his wine glass. She smiled at him and said lightly, "I hope I didn't disturb your illusions, *mon ami*. Naturally there are other marriages made without love but for less worldly reasons. Sometimes it is just a matter of companionship...."

Boardman nodded.

In the back of his mind he found himself wondering just why Helen was marrying him.

It was two days later that he caught Helen in an outright deception.

It happened late in the afternoon and by sheer accident. There had been tentative plans to drive out to Barbizon but at luncheon Helen had suddenly announced that she couldn't go.

"They telephoned from Patou's a few minutes ago that they expect me for some final fittings around four."

"Couldn't you postpone it until tomorrow?"

"Darling, how like a man! One doesn't postpone things with Patou. Particularly not if there's a rush to get things done."

Boardman nodded and let the matter drop.

But as a result he found himself without plans for the afternoon. He walked over to a brokerage office near the Bourse and spent the better part of an hour studying and opening quotations from the stock market in New York that were just beginning to come over the trans-Atlantic cable. After that there was nothing of particular interest to do.

He recalled then a semipromise he had made to Sam Hartley at the Harvard Club just before leaving New York. Sam's kid brother was supposed to be studying painting in Paris, although Sam expressed some doubts about it, saying, "The boy has got a right to have his fling if he wants it, but he's been over there for nearly two years now with nothing to show for it. I wish you'd drop in on him and make sure some French floozie hasn't got him on a string."

Now Boardman hunted through his card case for the address Hartley had given him. It was, he found, a number on the rue Delambre. A taxi took him across the Pont Neuf over to the Left Bank. The rue Delambre turned out to be a short, narrow street running diagonally from the intersection of the Boulevard Raspail and the Boulevard Montparnasse.

The house Boardman was looking for turned out to be a fairly modern studio-apartment building. In answer to his inquiries the concierge informed him that of a certainty M'sieu Hartley lived there but that at the moment he was not at home. It was possible he might be found at either the Dome or the Select or even in the American bar across the way.

Boardman paused on the sidewalk outside and debated whether to continue the search. After all, he had fulfilled his part of the errand Sam Hartley had wished on him. He had made an attempt to hunt up young Hartley and it wasn't his fault if the boy wasn't home. In a way it was just as well; he had no desire to stick his nose into affairs that were none of his business.

Nevertheless he crossed the street, telling himself he would have a quick drink and finish his search at one and the same time. He stood at the bar and ordered a Scotch and soda, trying not to notice the other Americans in the place. A weird bunch, he decided, looking as though they had been picked up bodily out of some Greenwich Village cellar dive and shipped overseas.

As he picked up his drink he glanced in the mirror behind the bar. He could see the reflection of the booths on the opposite side of the room and suddenly he paused with his glass half raised to his lips. The girl in the far booth, partially hidden in the embrace of the man beside her, reminded him surprisingly of Helen. For a moment he thought it was just the similarity of the hat and dress, but when she raised and half turned her head, he saw that it was more than that.

It *was* Helen!

He stood there fascinated for an endless moment, his eyes riveted on the arm that encircled Helen and the fingers that were slowly caressing her breast with the casual familiarity of an accepted lover. It was with an effort that he raised his eyes to look at the man's face. He was a stranger and yet not a stranger—Boardman had seen his counterpart a hundred times at the Claridge and Crillon and Ritz, usually dancing attendance to women with too many years and too much money.

A gigolo, he told himself, a goddamned gigolo!

Usually he was a man of direct action but now he found himself for some unknown reason curbing his first impulse to turn, stride across the room and confront the two. He simply didn't want to listen to the quick, facile explanations that he was certain Helen would be able to offer after the first speechless moment of shock.

He had listened to too many of her stories already.

He put his drink down untasted, slapped a twenty-franc note on the bar, and left.

In the taxi headed back across the river Boardman suddenly remembered that he had a dinner engagement with Helen and her mother for that night. Of one thing he was certain, he was in no mood to keep it now. Yet he could think of no easy way of getting out of it. If it had been with Helen alone that would have been one matter, but with Mrs. Avery he couldn't quite make the same brusque explanations.

He needed time to think things over.

He thought of something else then and leaned forward to tap on the driver's window and give the address of Patou.

While he was about it, he decided grimly, he might as well clear up everything.

The dinner was at Kaspec's, a new Russian place half way up Montmartre. The towering doorman was a Cossack general, the hat-check girl a Romanoff princess, and the waiters at least members of the minor nobility. In all likelihood, Boardman told himself as he tried to decipher the ornate script in which the menu was written, even the bus boy had a title.

Of one thing, however, he was thankful. There was somber entertainment of a sort and whenever this was going on the room was darkened. Then the only illumination consisted of a small amber spotlight on the entertainer of the moment and the ghostly glow of lights inset in the table gleaming just sufficiently through the tablecloths to mark the position of plates and glasses.

The shadowy darkness enabled him to let his mind work on the problem at hand without fear that his thoughts would be too clearly reflected on his face.

Helen chatted gaily and lightly and incessantly, skipping nervously from one subject to another. Boardman hoped that she would refrain from mentioning clothes and hats and appointments with couturiers in particular, but she didn't.

"And you should see what Patou is doing for me. It's simply out of this world!"

Boardman decided that now would be as good a time as any. He cleared his throat.

"Speaking of Patou, I had an idea this afternoon. I thought I would drop around there and settle up your account in advance. A surprise, you might say."

There was a moment's silence that Boardman could almost feel. Then Helen exclaimed, "But, Winnie, you can't! I mean, you mustn't even dream of a thing like that."

"But I—"

"Tell him, mother. Tell him that's the very last thing in the world he should do."

Somewhat hesitantly Mrs. Avery murmured, "Well, of course in my day it would hardly have been considered proper. But times have changed so...."

Helen cut in swiftly. "You see, Winnie. Even mother agrees with me. And it would be bad luck—frightfully bad luck!"

He knew damned well it would be bad luck, Boardman agreed silently. That much had already been proven to his satisfaction. And if Helen would only keep quiet long enough to let him finish what he had started to say she would find it out for herself.

"Promise Winnie! Promise you won't go near Patou." And then she managed a light laugh. "Good heavens, after we're married you'll have plenty of bills to pay. Why on earth should you want to start now—"

Boardman shrugged without answering. It was at that moment that the lights went up and as he turned his attention back to the food on his plate he was sharply aware of Helen's eyes studying him carefully.

She's worried, he told himself. Well, damn it, she ought to be worried!

He was tempted to go on, to have a showdown then and there. But he remembered the presence of Mrs. Avery in time. After all, there was no point in making a liar out of Helen in front of her mother.

Plans had been nebulous for the remainder of the evening, but now suddenly Helen had ideas.

"Let's make a round of the night clubs, Winnie. The really gay ones, I mean. Do you know I've never been to Zelli's or Bricktop's or the Florida?"

Boardman sought for an excuse. "I don't think your mother ..."

"Oh, but mother can't go with us. She's been complaining of a headache all day. Haven't you, darling?"

Mrs. Avery looked a bit uncertain, as though not quite certain of her cue. "Headache? Well, of course, it has been a trying day...."

Boardman tried to keep his face expressionless. He wondered just how much she knew or suspected of her daughter's activities. Unless she were utterly blind, as blind as he had permitted himself to be, she must be aware that Helen was up to something.

After dinner they dropped Mrs. Avery at the hotel and then drove back up the hill to the Montmartre section. Helen was almost deliberately, recklessly gay. She drank considerably more than was her custom; when they danced her pliant body pressed closely against his, her firm thighs rubbing with a disturbing intimacy against his legs. At the table she was constantly touching him with her hands.

Once she chided half laughingly, "You're not very responsive tonight, Winnie. Can't you forget whatever it is you're worrying about for a little while?"

He wasn't worried about anything, Boardman told her. "It's simply that I'm waiting to have a talk with you. There are certain things that have to be cleared up."

"But not tonight, darling! Tonight let's just forget everything and be gay."

Boardman shook his head. "I'm no good at pretending, Helen. I'm no good at hiding things, either. I started to tell you at dinner and then decided not to because of your mother's presence. But I wasn't just thinking about going to Patou this afternoon. I went there."

There was a moment's silence. Then Helen laughed. "Poor Winnie! And you discovered that I didn't have anything ordered there at all. Is that it?"

"Partly."

"But, darling, you men never understand. Women always say they're going to Patou or Lanvin or some other frightfully expensive couturier when really it's to some clever little dress-maker on a side street who copies the very same designs at a fifth the price. But we all try to keep it a secret." She reached over and put a hand on his arm. "You should be happy you're not getting an extravagant woman, darling!"

Boardman gave his head a brusk shake. "That wasn't quite all that happened." He paused, mentally picking his words carefully so that there would be no mistake in how it had come about. "Sam Hartley asked me to look up his younger brother if I had time. The boy lives over on the Left Bank, on the rue Delambre. I went over there this afternoon but he wasn't in. So I stopped in the bar across the way for a drink. The Dingo it was called, if I remember right. Hell of a name for a bar." He paused again, then finished in a flat voice, "You were there, Helen."

This time her silence was longer. Her fingertips, which had been stroking the back of his hand, became motionless. And her laugh, when at last it came, had a brittle thinness.

"Really, darling, I don't understand. You saw me and didn't speak?"

"You were with some one."

"But of course." Her words came out now in a quick, nervous rush. "I was on the same sort of errand you were. I'd promised Celeste Kiffer to look up her brother here and I had a few minutes to spare and—" She broke off and laughed again. "Darling, don't tell me you were jealous!"

Oh, for God's sake! Boardman thought wearily. Just how much of a fool does she take me for, anyway? Does she think for a moment that I didn't see the man's arm about her and his hands caressing her breast and the way she was enjoying it? But I suppose if I mentioned it she'd have an excuse for that, too.

And it was ridiculous to suggest that he had been jealous. Shocked and outraged, yes. But jealousy implied the reaction of emotions he was relieved to discover he didn't possess. Not as far as Helen was concerned, at any rate.

"No," he said slowly. "I wasn't jealous."

"You see, darling? If you'd only asked me in the beginning I could have explained everything so simply."

"So I see."

Something in the tone of his voice made her glance at him again sharply, as though not quite certain of his real meaning. He busied himself lighting a cigarette and then turning his attention to the floor show. A light brownskinned girl whose costume consisted of a cluster of three strategically placed bananas was engaged in a wild African dance that left little doubt as to its phallic symbolism. Pretending an interest he didn't feel, Boardman said casually, "Amazing, isn't she? I saw her this morning walking down the Rue de la Paix leading a pet leopard. And I understand that less than a year ago she was just an unknown chorus girl up in some Harlem club."

"I think she's disgusting!" Helen snapped. "She makes everything much too obvious. Let's go somewhere else, shall we?"

It was toward three in the morning when Helen finally suggested that they call it a night. In the taxi headed back to the hotel, she relaxed against Boardman, letting her body curve softly and invitingly in a half-completed embrace.

He pretended not to notice.

She sighed faintly against his shoulder. "You're much too sober, Winnie. And I've had much too much to drink."

He murmured something deliberately vague in reply and glanced out of the window. The taxi was just swinging about in front of the Crillon.

The Averys had rooms two floors above the suite occupied by Boardman. He was prepared to say good night in the elevator, but Helen suddenly had a different idea.

"I want another drink, Winnie. Can't we have a nightcap?"

"I think the bar is closed by now."

"Haven't you anything in your room?"

He lied automatically. "Not at the moment."

"Then have something sent up." She turned and spoke swiftly in French to the elevator attendant. "It is possible to have some wine sent up to M'sieu Boardman's room, is it not?"

"Oui, madame."

"You see, darling, how simple everything is if you only know how."

Boardman opened his mouth to protest and then thought better of it. The elevator had already stopped at his floor, the door was open and Helen was ahead of him walking down the hallway toward his suite.

He frowned slightly as he unlocked the door, wondering what the hell was up now. More facile explanations, most likely. She probably was aware that he hadn't believed a word she had said earlier and so now had a new story to offer.

But whatever she said wouldn't make any difference.

He watched her speculatively as she lit a cigarette and moved aimlessly about the room, stopping at last to study her reflection in the ornate mirror over the marble mantelpiece of the fireplace.

"I do look a little the worse for wear, don't I?" she murmured over her shoulder. "I think I'd like to use your little girl's room."

He noticed that she swayed slightly as she walked through the bedroom toward the bath, and wondered just how drunk she really was. At the same time he wondered how long it would be before he could get rid of her. He was tired and annoyed and wanted more than anything to get to bed and asleep.

With rest and a clear head in the morning he could face what had to be done.

There was a discreet rap on the hall door and the waiter appeared with champagne in an ice bucket.

"Shall I open it, m'sieu?"

Boardman nodded, eying the wine with displeasure. Under the best of circumstances he wasn't fond of champagne; as far as he was concerned it was a drink without body or substance, always too sweet or too dry, but either way inclined to leave a fuzzy aftermath in the morning.

As the door closed behind the departing waiter Helen reappeared.

"Pour me a drink, darling. You're really not being an attentive host."

When he handed her the glass she stood in front of him, waiting, the drink half raised to her lips. Then when he made no move she protested with a little laugh, "But where's your glass? There should be a toast, shouldn't there?"

Boardman said quietly, "Should there?"

"But, of course." She raised the glass until she could just look over the top into his eyes. "A toast—to us."

"That's something for us to talk about later."

"Talk!" she cried. She put down her glass and moved closer until her body was touching his. "Words! Can't you realize there's a time when words aren't needed, darling...."

He glanced down at her uncomfortable nearness. He hadn't noticed before that her evening dress was cut so low or revealed quite so much. With a fragment of his mind he wondered if she had rearranged her clothes somehow while in the bathroom. He would have noticed before if her breasts had been half exposed the way they were now.

Her arms went about his neck as her face turned up toward his. Her voice became a throaty whisper. "You aren't very romantic, are you, Winnie?"

He tried to keep his tone level. "Look, Helen, you've had a lot to drink and—"

She stopped him with a laugh. "And you're protecting me from myself. Is that it? I've only had enough to drink to know what I want, Winnie." She raised her lips until they were brushing against his and her words were almost too low to hear. "We don't have to wait, darling. We don't have to wait for anything...."

He felt like a fool standing there motionless. Yesterday or the day before he might have responded, but not now. On top of that the whole business had an air of unreality.

"You don't know what you're saying, Helen. Suppose you finish your drink and run along to bed."

She repeated his last words in a singsong fashion. "To bed, to bed. But that's what I've been trying to tell you, darling. That's where I want to go. But not alone ..."

She stepped back and swirled away from him. One strap of her evening dress had slipped from her shoulder, exposing the firm roundness of a breast, the upper half deeply tanned in startling contrast to the creamy white flesh below. She laughed over her shoulder at Boardman as she half turned and deliberately lowered the other strap.

The bodice of her dress cascaded about her hips, leaving her nude from the waist up, as she faced Boardman again.

"Don't you like me this way, darling? Do you think I'd make a nice South Sea island girl with just a sarong about my hips?"

As she spoke her fingers were busy with hooks and fastenings and suddenly the dress fell in a crumpled circle of chiffon and silk about her ankles. "Or like this, darling? Tell me I have as nice a figure as that African dancer you stared at so. Tell me!"

She stepped clear of the discarded dress encircling her feet. Except for sheer silk stockings upheld by black garters decorated with blue rosettes and high-heeled evening slippers, she was completely naked. Even as he stared at her Boardman thought mechanically, I was right, after all. She did rearrange her clothes in the bathroom, getting rid of whatever she was wearing underneath that dress.

She had this damned business in mind all along.

And as she moved slowly toward him he realized something else with sharp clarity. The moment he reached out and took hold of her, the moment they were in bed together, then at that very moment all her lies and deceptions would be automatically balanced. Wiped out.

More than that, he would become the one in the wrong. Whatever the real truth, he was willing to bet a thousand to one that afterward she would adroitly blame him for taking advantage of her, seducing her when she was too drunk to know what she was doing.

And she knows damned well what she's doing, he thought bitterly. She probably planned the whole thing from the moment at dinner when he let her know that he was on to her lies.

That explained why she had got rid of her mother on the pretense of the latter having a headache and then insisted on making a round of the night clubs. Laying the groundwork for just what was happening now.

She had closed the little distance that separated them and now she was standing with her body touching his again. Once more her arms crept up about his neck. She bent back at the waist so that she could stare up into his face, while at the same time her bare hips pressed with searching intimacy against him.

She whispered, "Why are we waiting, darling? There's nothing to be afraid of...."

Her mouth was against his then, kissing him passionately. All the tricks, he thought coldly, she knows all the tricks. Maybe she learned them from the gigolo she was with this afternoon. Maybe she always knew them....

With a quick, sudden movement he reached up and tore her clinging arms away.

"For God's sake, Helen, snap out of it! Put your dress on and behave yourself!"

"But, darling...."

"It's no good, I tell you. I'm not having any."

She stood there in the center of the room, swaying slightly, staring at him through half-closed eyes as he crossed over to the table and picked up his wine glass and emptied it with one quick swallow. She ran her hands in a deliberately provocative caress over her bare breasts and hips and then gave a pleased laugh.

"I think you really are afraid of me, darling. Or is it of yourself?"

"Stop talking nonsense!"

"Why don't we just stop talking, darling?" She advanced toward him again, seeking once more to capture him with her body. Boardman waited with mounting anger until she was close enough and then with a sudden gesture slapped her across the face with the flat of his hand.

She stumbled back against a chair, holding one hand to her smarting cheek, her eyes wide with shock.

"You hit me, Winnie...."

"Damn it, of course I hit you! Can't you get it through your head that I don't want you.... That I don't want any part of you. Now will you please get the hell out!"

Her eyes hardened as she glared back at him.

"You needn't be such a damned prude! Just because I'm honest enough to admit having human emotions...."

He cut her short. "Stop lying! Don't you suppose I know where you were this afternoon and what you were doing? Hell, you were both so busy making love that you didn't have eyes for anything else. Otherwise you might have seen me when I came into the bar. And now you've got the bright idea that everything will be fine if you just crawl into bed with me. I told you before—I'm not having any. Not now or any time!"

She said slowly, "You filthy-minded son-of-a-bitch."

Boardman shrugged wearily. "Maybe. Now are you going to put on your dress and walk out under your own steam, or shall I throw you out into the hall and your clothes after you?"

She moved slowly, purposely flaunting her nakedness before his eyes, taking her time picking up her dress from the floor and sliding it over her body. When she was clothed at last she went over to the mirror and studied her reflection carefully, patting her hair back into place and cleaning the smudged lipstick from her mouth with the corner of a handkerchief.

She turned about at last.

"You're worse than a prude, Winnie. You're a fool, a stupid fool, as well. God knows what kind of a woman you think you want but you'll never find her, my friend. You've about as much romance and warmth as a dead mackerel. Whoever marries you will marry you only for your money and she'll find her romance somewhere else. On that you can count, Winnie. Women will always cheat on you!"

In a tired voice Boardman said, "Get out before I slap you down again."

She shrugged and walked over to the door.

As she opened it and went out Boardman noticed mechanically that she was no longer pretending to be partly drunk.

The bitch, he said to himself heavily.

CHAPTER SEVEN

L ATE IN THE morning Mrs. Avery telephoned him. Her voice had the same plaintive appeal that he had become familiar with when she used to call him at his office.

And her words were nearly the same.

"I wonder if I could see you for a few moments alone, Winthrop. I—It's rather important."

He had no desire to see Mrs. Avery. God alone knew what Helen had told her. Certainly not the truth. And he didn't feel like explanations or emotional scenes.

He heard her speaking again against his silence.

"If you're not busy now, Winthrop, I could step down to your room.…"

He lied quickly and easily. "I'm sorry, but there are some people here now." He hesitated, realizing that sooner or later he would have to see her. "I could meet you for luncheon, however. At the Vendome at one?"

It was a moment before Mrs. Avery agreed. Boardman had a feeling that she would have preferred a more private rendezvous. But that was just what he had every intention of avoiding.

Although he was two minutes early Mrs. Avery was already waiting for him when he appeared. She gave him her usual wistful little smile of helplessness.

"I hope I didn't tear you away from something important, Winthrop."

"Not at all."

At the table she declined a cocktail. She stared at the menu blankly, clearly unable to concentrate on food, and nodded vaguely to the first suggestion the hovering head-waiter made.

"I really haven't any appetite at all," she explained to Boardman in her plaintive voice. "I never have when things upset me."

Boardman said politely, "I'm sorry you're not feeling well."

"Oh, it's nothing physical. It's just—well, nervousness. I'm *so* senstive to the atmosphere about me. And when things go wrong—" She broke off and glanced at him quickly and then hurried on, "Things like this childish misunderstanding between you and Helen. Of course, I *know* it's nothing serious but still ..."

Her words trailed off, waiting for him to give her some encouragement. Instead he said flatly, "I'm afraid it isn't a misunderstanding, Mrs. Avery. It's something quite definite and complete."

"But Winthrop, you can't really mean that!" And then, as though aware too late of the sharpness of her cry, she went on in a softer tone, "I mean, after all it is rather hasty, isn't it? Sometimes Helen is thoughtless and—and too impulsive, like all young girls today. Of course, I don't know what all this is about—"

She broke off as the waiter appeared and went through the ritual of serving a filet of sole with a simple sauce meunière. She poked at it tentatively with her fork and then glanced up at Boardman again.

"As I say, I don't know what it's actually all about. But I'm certain it's just an unfortunate misunderstanding that can be straightened out."

Just how much did she know, Boardman wondered. How much had Helen told her and how much did she suspect? He had an idea that she had been aware of what Helen was up to long before he had stumbled on the truth.

He said flatly, "I'm sorry, Mrs. Avery. I'm afraid talking won't do any good."

He saw that the hand holding her fork was trembling. She put it down carefully and fumbled in her handbag for a wisp of lace handkerchief. Her face had become drawn and white so that the little spots of rouge on her cheekbones stood out vividly.

When she spoke again it was in hesitant, disjointed phrases. "It's all so confusing.... I don't know what to do. All the plans made and everything. It's going to be very difficult...."

Something clicked in Boardman's mind. He was remembering Helen's taunting remark flung at him in cold anger—the kind of cold anger that sometimes carries the truth with it. "Whoever marries you will only marry you for your money." And at the same moment he recalled something else—the rumor that at the time of his death old John Avery had been in serious financial trouble and that the estate he left had been a small one. More than one person had wondered how Mrs. Avery managed to continue living on the scale she did without dipping heavily into her capital.

He looked at her thoughtfully. "Just how difficult will it be, Mrs. Avery?"

She made a small, helpless gesture. "I've been very foolish, I'm afraid. The trousseau and this trip and everything ... I really shouldn't have—"

Boardman demanded bluntly, "Just how much are you in debt?"

She made a final pretense. "Really, Winthrop, I don't see why I should bother you with my little worries...."

"How much?"

"Well—it's a lot, I'm afraid. I've been foolishly extravagant but I was thinking only of Helen. I wanted her to have only the best...."

Boardman said patiently, "I understand all that, Mrs. Avery. But just how much does it all amount to?"

She managed her wistfully appealing little smile. "I'm no good at all on figures, Winthrop. But I think—I'm almost certain—that it's around eighteen or twenty thousand. Though why you should want to know...."

He was only half listening to her. Perhaps it was better this way, he decided as he drew out his check book. This would remove the whole sordid business from the misleading status of a broken romance and make it definitely what it had clearly been from the start—a commercial proposition.

He signed the check, tore it loose from its stub, and, reaching across the table, placed it beside her plate. He noticed that she took a quick glance down at the amount before she went into a mild flurry of feeble protests.

"But, Winthrop, you shouldn't do this! I mean, I shouldn't let you.... And for twenty-five thousand—"

He didn't want to hear any more. "That's quite all right, Mrs. Avery. In a way I was to blame for some of your extravagances. You shouldn't be called on to pay for the mistakes of others."

And it would have been cheap at double the price, he told himself. At least he had found out in time before embarking on a marriage that would likely have wound up in Reno and cost him far more in money and damaged pride. True enough, he was under no moral obligation to bail the Averys out of debt, but it was a gesture he could afford.

He wondered suddenly if by chance Helen had been correct, and that it would always be only his money that would attract women.

And in the same moment he thought of Yvonne.

She was a whore and as such an outcast from the tight social orbit in which Helen and her mother moved and had their being.

But she was certainly a damned sight less hypocritical and far more honest. So far she had refused any gift from him, permitting him only to pay the set fees of the house arranged by Madame Romain.

"You are with me as a friend and not as a client," she had reminded him. "And one does not charge for friendship...."

As he listened to Mrs. Avery's voice fluttering on and waited impatiently to pay the luncheon check, he reflected sardonically on the moral chasm separating Yvonne and the Averys. The latter were willing enough to accept money for nothing—the former, with pride in her profession, wanted payment only for services rendered.

As far as he was concerned the balance was all on Yvonne's side.

CHAPTER EIGHT

YVONNE STARED HARD at Boardman again and then gave her head a quick little shake as though to free herself from a web of puzzled thoughts.

"But surely you can't be serious! You are acting now on impulse, my friend."

"It's not an impulse. I've thought it over very carefully."

"But it is still fantastic. It is only because you are not thinking clearly that you do not see it. You have been hurt and disappointed and so now you are acting on what you call the rebound. You are angry because you discovered your fiancée was having an affair with one man. But I—" She paused and spread her hands out. "Think of how many affairs, how many men I have had, *mon ami*. It is my life—it has been my profession since I was fifteen years old."

"It was a business," Boardman said. "You weren't living under false pretenses. You were deceiving no one."

Yvonne smiled faintly. "You speak as though it were all in the past."

"It is if I can make it that way." He leaned forward in his chair, once again repeating the arguments he had already used. "I'm not an impetuous boy, Yvonne. I'm twenty-eight and know quite well what I want. That's why I became engaged to Helen in the first place—because I wanted a home and children. But I want a wife who is anxious for the same things and one whom I can trust without thinking about it. As I can trust you. You told me once you entered this sort of life only because you wanted money and security for the future. It's because you have a sense of values that you've succeeded in rising to the top while a thousand others who started as you did are taking the easiest way into landing nowhere. I think you'd have the same sense of values in your own home and in a different environment."

"But surely you could find some girl in your own class—"

Boardman cut her short with a brusk laugh. "Helen is a good example of girls of my class, as you call it. Better than most, to be honest. All any of them care about is having their own way with some man to foot the bills."

"And you believe I would be different?"

He nodded. "I think you would be just as successful as a wife as you have been—Well, as you have been here. It would be a matter of pride with you."

Yvonne sighed and drew her fingertips lightly across her eyes. "You make me a little dizzy, my friend, with so many words and so many strange ideas. And you ask so much. It is not something that can be answered in a moment."

"I didn't expect it would be."

She smiled at him then and said with soft mockery, "There is only one argument you have failed to mention. You spoke of honesty and trust and respect. But isn't there supposed to be romance in marriage, as well?"

Boardman shrugged. "I was warned not to expect that. I was told plainly enough that I would be married for my money and no other reason."

Yvonne looked at him thoughtfully for a long moment and then shook her head. "Never believe what a woman says in anger, my friend. It is not always the truth but only what it is hoped might be true...."

"Perhaps. But I've already made one mistake. I don't care to lay myself open to another."

The glance that Yvonne gave him still held a hint of protective mockery. "And I, too, my friend," she said softly. "I, too, must protect myself against mistakes."

She had been half reclining, half sitting in a chaise longue across the room from Boardman but now she stood up and walked toward the table holding the wine bucket. She was wearing a negligee of pale chiffon and when she moved the thin material molded itself smoothly about the slender perfection of her body. Looking at her, Boardman felt his blood quicken. She was a damned good-looking woman! Who said there wouldn't be romance, or the next thing to it, in such a marriage....

It was almost as though she were reading his mind when she stopped in front of him to refill his glass and murmured lightly, "You speak of marriage, *mon ami,* which is the ultimate intimacy. Yet in the numerous times you have been here you have made no attempt to take what you could have without question. That is a curious thing, is it not?"

Boardman shook his head.

"Not under the circumstances. Sex can be bought anywhere. I preferred to think of you differently. And now I'm just as glad things happened as they did." He took a sip of his wine and laughed. "At least you know that it isn't raw passion that prompts me to make my offer now."

Yvonne looked down at him quietly and smiled. She wondered if he really knew what was prompting him.

Americans were strange creatures....

Later, when he had left and she had retired for what remained of the night, she found herself unable to sleep—unable to rid her mind of this curious American and his unexpected proposal.

Fantastic as the idea was, in a way it was easy to understand. It was motivated by a combination of damaged pride and fear—fear that such a thing could easily happen to him again. That, more than anything, was doubtlessly why he could now entertain so readily the thought of marrying a woman of her profession.

Fearing disillusion, he had the naïve idea that he could protect himself by starting with no illusions at all.

She had heard it said often enough that American men were slaves to their wives. To her that had always seemed a preposterous exaggeration—it was hard to believe that men who were so forcefully dominant and aggressive in business could be at the same time weak and vacillating in their own homes, in the very place where they should be masters.

The truth was, she supposed, that they simply did not understand women. Beneath the veneer of their practical materialism they were hopelessly romantic and sentimental, making a too-good-to-be-true ideal out of their womenfolk and then becoming subservient to the false image they had created. That was probably why most of them still suffered from an almost juvenile complex in sexual matters, unable to rid themselves of a sense of guilt.

She had long since noticed that most of the Americans who visited the establishment had usually had a good deal to drink earlier and that they continued to drink up to the very moment of making love. As though sex were a sister dissipation to intoxication, and not an art to be delicately and knowingly savored.

And that was another strange thing—the words and phrases they used sometimes in an attempt to cloak a purely physical act in a misty veil of sentimentality. Making love, they called it. *Making love.* But what had love to do with the momentary possession of a purchased body—what had love to do with an act that was as instinctive as breathing?

She wondered then if possibly that explained in part the hold that American women had over their men. Had they somehow sold them the idea that they only gave themselves for "love"—that it was only "love" and not a natural excitement and desire that made them active partners in passion?

If this were true, no wonder that this strange American, this M'sieu Boardman, was trying to break away from the pattern.

Still, his suggestion of marriage was fantastic. In her mind she had the future so clearly mapped out. So many years more at her profession, with her money securely invested in small properties that returned a safe interest. Then, when the time came that her charms began to fade and the demand for her professional services lessened, she would have sufficient to purchase a small inn in some quiet village not too far from Paris.

Safety and security, with no worries of any importance. Possibly even a husband and children, if it wasn't too late for the latter.

And thinking of marriage she thought again of Boardman and his proposal. It was a clear waste of time letting her mind dwell on anything so impractical and illogical, she told herself sleepily.

Still …

CHAPTER NINE

LATE IN THE morning Madame Romain sought Yvonne out.

"What passes with this American of yours?" she demanded without preamble. "Have you completely bewitched him?"

"Why?"

"At an unearthly hour this morning he telephoned, insisting on speaking to me. He wished to engage your services exclusively for an indefinite period." She gave a little shrug of annoyance. "If he feels that way, why doesn't he set you up in an apartment in the proper manner?"

Yvonne smiled. "I suggested as much but it seems that he has other ideas." She paused and then added slowly, "He wishes to marry me."

Madame Romain stared at her blankly. "Marry! But you are joking. Why should a man of such wealth marry a whore? It is without reason."

"Most certainly. But nevertheless he is very persistent in his arguments." Briefly she recounted the things he had told her and added her own impressions. "In a way, you see, it is easy to understand...."

Madame Romain clucked her tongue against her teeth in a sharp exclamation. "*Incroyable!* I have often wondered which are the more to be pitied—the men such as this American who know too little about women or the others who know too much. They both miss a great deal." She shrugged again and eyed Yvonne speculatively. "And you—what have you told this lost one?"

"That the idea is impractical."

"Why?"

"Why did I tell him?"

"No. Why is the idea impractical? This Boardman is a man of wealth, but his desires appear to be simple. Such a one is easy for a clever woman to handle."

"But I don't wish to spend the remainder of my life being clever," Yvonne protested. "I have other plans for the future when I retire."

"You misunderstand me. I didn't mean the cleverness of the demimondaine. I meant the cleverness to be an intelligent wife. It is a skill that many women have obviously forgotten else our profession wouldn't be so successful." She paused and then ticked the advantages off on her fingers. "A home, security, a husband of means. What more do you expect to find in this world?"

"And later when he has regrets? When he remembers and reminds me that he took me out of a brothel?"

Madame Romain spread her hands out. "That is something to be handled when the time comes. But if you are wise in the way you handle him why should he ever have regrets?"

"Most husbands do, don't they?" Yvonne suggested. "I have listened to the confidences of a good many married men in my time and they all tell much the same story. Only the reasons vary."

"Bah!" snapped Madame Romain impatiently. "Such regrets are only excuses they make themselves for being unfaithful. Or being natural, as you prefer."

She got up and started for the door and then paused and glanced back over her shoulder at Yvonne.

"I should regret, myself, to lose you, but I like to see my girls advance themselves. It speaks well for the house."

"But I haven't decided as yet."

"You will," Madame Romain told her with a positive nod of the head. "After all, you have everything to gain and nothing to lose."

Madame wasn't quite correct, Yvonne decided as the day wore on. It was true enough that from a material standpoint there would be much to gain from a marriage to Boardman, but there would be other things that could be lost, as well.

There were moral principles involved. Being a whore—giving her body for money—was one thing. In this world one had to gain one's livelihood in whatever manner presented itself. In that there was nothing to be ashamed of. But giving one's self in marriage was another matter entirely.

She tried to explain it to Boardman when he appeared early in the evening.

"It is a serious matter, my friend. I would be happy enough to become your mistress, if that is your wish. But marriage—" She paused briefly and then shrugged helplessly as though not too sure of the force of her own arguments. "Marriage is not a gesture to be made thoughtlessly."

"I don't intend it to be," Boardman said bluntly.

He was surprised to find himself growing increasingly stubborn at Yvonne's resistance. The fact that she would have no hesitancy in living with him but drew back doubtfully from the respectable security of marriage seemed incredible. He would have thought she would jump at the chance.

As Helen had jumped....

And once again he was impressed with Yvonne's seriousness and honesty. Certainly no one could ever say that she had led him on to make a fool of himself. On the contrary, she was doing her best to discourage him.

He came back to the idea that had brought him to the house at such an early hour.

Now he made the suggestion. "I thought we might go out somewhere to dinner. And afterward for dancing at some club, if you like."

She gave a resigned sigh. "You see, my friend? You have forgotten that in the places we might go there would undoubtedly be gentlemen, clients of the house, who would recognize me. For myself it does not matter, but for you it would be embarrassing."

"We could go to some quiet, out-of-the-way place."

She laughed. "And there we would most certainly be found out." She turned and walked over to the mirror and studied her reflection for a long moment. When she spoke it was as though she were speaking to herself rather than Boardman. "It would take time to arrange it so that such things could be done without exciting comment. A slight difference in the hair, perhaps, and the way it is done. And a change in make-up. Enough to alter the personality...."

"Your personality is all right," Boardman said. "I wouldn't want you to change it. Just your name, that's all."

She turned to face him and smiled a little. "I have changed it before. It is really Marie—or had you forgotten that?"

He had forgotten nothing, he told her. "Tomorrow when you walk out of here you'll leave Yvonne behind. You'll become Marie again. Not the one you ran away from in Normandy, but a new one."

Yvonne shook her head and gave a mock sigh of resignation. "You are very impetuous, my friend."

"Not at all. I simply know what I want."

CHAPTER TEN

THEY ARRIVED IN New York on board the *Ile de France* some two months later.

The intervening time had gone almost too swiftly for Marie. There had been so many changes to be made, changes of habit that were mental as well as physical. Even such a simple matter as becoming accustomed to the use of her own name once again.

It had been a long time since she had thought of herself as Marie. And it was a name she had never wanted to use again, for it reminded her too poignantly of Laverny and the bleak, crude poverty of her childhood. But it was the name that had been used to register her birth and hence of necessity had to appear on the marriage license and later the passport.

Only it was no longer Marie Courcel. It was Marie Courcel Boardman.

That made a difference.

There had been other abrupt changes, as well. In the beginning Boardman had tried to insist on an immediate marriage, almost an elopement, but she had refused to be rushed off of her feet. She needed a space of time to adjust herself, she had told him. But that had been a pretense—actually it had been the idea of moving directly from a brothel bed to a bridal bed that had shocked her.

There should be an appropriate interval, she felt, at least sufficient to make the change apparent.

They had been married exactly one month after the day she left the Maison d'Or. After seeing her established in a discreet family hotel just off the Champs Elysées, Boardman had made a hurried trip to New York, remaining there less than a fortnight.

"I hadn't planned to be away this long," he explained. "I want to arrange things at the office to be away another six weeks or so. And I want to make sure the new house will be ready for us when we get to Old Haven."

"Of course," Marie agreed. Then a random thought intruded. "Does your family yet know of your new plans?"

"There's only my mother. She's at Bar Harbor for the summer, but I'll run up there for a week end." He paused and looked at her thoughtfully, and then added half jokingly, "I hope you won't change your mind while I'm away."

"I won't," Marie promised.

She had utilized the days of his absence in preparing herself for her new life. She made deft changes in her appearance. Her hair, which she had always worn long, she had cut into the fashionable bob of the moment. She stopped using mascara and eye shadow to emphasize the violet blueness of her eyes and altered the way she did her mouth. Each change was slight, yet added together they were sufficient to cause anyone who had only known her casually—or in the Maison d'Or—to doubt if she were the same person.

Five days after Boardman's return to Paris the marriage ceremony took place. That was in the late morning and immediately afterward they set out on a leisurely motor trip through the south of France.

They spent the first night in a hotel in Avignon.

Marie had been surprised to find herself actually nervous as she contemplated the approaching moment of intimacy. It was a feeling that was new to her—one that she hadn't even entertained that first time, in the house of Madame Gerlaine, when she was only fifteen. Then, as she remembered it, she had felt only curiosity and a certain eagerness born of ignorance.

But now the fact of being married changed everything. An act that she had performed a thousand times without thinking twice about it, either before or afterward, now took on a special significance.

She was aware of an almost virginal embarrassment.

It was late when they reached Avignon and went up to their room. Apparently Boardman felt an awkwardness, too, Marie decided, for almost immediately he suggested sending down for champagne.

"After all, we skipped having a wedding party in Paris. We should celebrate here."

But not with champagne, Marie thought quickly. Champagne was a little too much like the Maison d'Or.

"If you don't mind, I'd rather have sherry," she said casually. "A dry sherry, if they have it."

While he was seeing about the order she took her overnight bag into the bathroom. It wasn't modesty that prompted her desire for privacy—simply the fact that she had undressed before too many men during her professional life.

And that profession was now part of the past.

As she bathed and then dried and powdered her body she thought of the other changes that would have to take place. Certain instinctive habits would be hard to break. She could no longer let her mind deliberately wander while her body was possessed, carefully keeping her own emotions from leading her into a reciprocal excitement. Now there would be no need to guard her sexual vitality or fear exhaustion.

And she smiled inwardly as she thought, Perhaps now for the first time I can actually enjoy being with a man.

She put on a nightgown of lace and sheer blue silk and a matching negligee. She gave a final appraising glance at herself in the bathroom mirror and then turned and re-entered the bedroom.

Boardman had already undressed. Clad only in his shorts, he was sitting on the edge of the bed, smoking a cigarette and sipping at the brandy and soda he had finally ordered.

He held up his glass as Marie came into the room. "I hope you don't mind that I didn't wait for you. But I needed a pickup after that long drive." He got up and went over to the table and poured out a glass of sherry. As he handed it to her his eyes swept quickly over her body.

"You're a damned beautiful woman, Marie!"

She smiled at him. "Thank you. That's something you never told me before. And every woman likes to hear it, whether it is true or not...."

"It's true, all right. But I'm no good at making pretty speeches." He went back to the bed with his glass. "Come sit beside me while you finish your drink."

She moved over to the bed, propping the pillows against the headboard, half reclining as she sipped her sherry and waited.

It was only a moment and he was removing the glass from her fingers and his hands, heavy and impatient, were on her shoulders, drawing her closer.

His mouth was firm and demanding as it bruised against her lips and then his hands, seeking to find their way beneath the lace and silk of her robe, became awkward with haste.

"Wait," she whispered against his eagerness. "Just one little moment, please...."

She shrugged free of the negligee and let it fall to the floor beside the bed. Now there was just the silken sheath of her nightgown to delay him, silk that slid smoothly upward over her flesh.

She wished that the light had been turned off first....

She closed her eyes and tried to make her mind and her body receptive. It was hard to know where the habit of passionate pretense ended and the awakening of honest emotions began. For Boardman was not a practiced nor a subtle lover; he was concerned primarily with his own desire and his own satisfaction. He was intense and powerful, but it was an intensity and power that burned itself out quickly.

When it was over Marie remained quiet, holding his head against her cheek, her fingers lightly caressing his muscular shoulders.

And she thought, Perhaps it was just as well that I was not a virgin, not a beginner. Otherwise I would have been disappointed.

Perhaps, too, that is why so many American marriages end badly. Because they start with disappointment and frustration....

Boardman raised his head and looked down into her eyes.

"Are you happy, honey?"

"Yes," she told him softly. "Very happy, my dear...."

The honeymoon passed quickly. Marie would have been content to remain in one place, but Boardman possessed a nervous energy that kept them constantly on the move. Although in theory they were touring places of historic interest she discovered soon enough that he had little patience in viewing cathedrals or museums or ancient castles. He was happiest where he could engage in some form of physical activity, playing golf or tennis or swimming. He still had a juvenile pride in excelling at sports.

In the beginning he was half apologetic about leaving her to her own devices.

"I'd like to try out the golf course at Monte Carlo," he would say. "I've been told it's something pretty special." Or it might be that some chance acquaintance had invited him to the tennis club in Nice. "You're sure you don't mind if I leave you for a bit?"

Shaking her head, Marie smiled. "But of course not. The exercise will do you good."

"But what will you find to do?"

"I have books to read and a bit of embroidery to work on." She kissed him lightly on the lips and patted his cheek. "Run along and enjoy yourself."

In a way she welcomed those periods of privacy. For the first time she was realizing the luxury of being very nearly her own mistress. Always before she had been at the beck and call of some one, first on the farm in Laverny and later at the house of Madame Gerlaine and the Maison d'Or. There she had never been free from interruptions; either it was the other girls of the house intent on an exchange of professional gossip or a client arriving at some unaccustomed hour.

Always, it seemed, she had been constantly on parade, constantly on exhibition, having to pretend a mood of lightness and gaiety whether she felt it or not.

Now, to a certain extent, she could be herself. Even during the intransigeance of the honeymoon her life was beginning to fit into a formal pattern.

She was well content.

And Winthrop was clearly a man without complications. His tastes and his reactions to the world about him were simple and direct.

He would be easy to manage....

CHAPTER ELEVEN

S HE HAD BEEN hesitant about her reception in Old Haven.
It was Boardman's home town and the people there were family friends of long standing. That his sudden and unexpected marriage to an unknown French girl had excited talk and curiosity went without saying. Marie knew that she would be critically watched and judged.

Winthrop seemed blandly unaware that there would be any possible problems. It was early September when they arrived in Old Haven; the new house was finished but not yet furnished. "It will keep you busy the next few weeks getting everything in order," Boardman told her. "I'll have Blaisdell get in touch with you right away."

"But who is Blaisdell?"

"The interior decorator who does most of the important jobs around here. He's supposed to be one of the best."

Marie frowned faintly. "You mean it is this Blaisdell who selects the furnishings and things and decides where and how they should be put?"

"That's right. All you'll have to do is to see that he keeps up to schedule."

The frown on Marie's forehead deepened. "But this is to be our home, is it not? And a home is a private place. Why should a stranger tell us how we should arrange it?"

Boardman stared at her blankly for a moment and then laughed. "Damned if I know! It's just that everybody always calls in an interior decorator whenever it's a question of furnishing a couple of rooms. Habit, I guess. Or maybe just damned laziness."

Meantime, until their own home was ready, they were staying at the old Boardman place. Winthrop's mother had come down from Bar Harbor to be on hand to greet them. She made no effort to conceal her frank curiosity.

"I may as well tell you right now," she informed Marie. "I'm still mystified about the whole business. The first inkling I had was when he came up to Maine to see me and announced out of the clear sky that he was marrying some French girl he'd never even mentioned before. It was all the more amazing because Winthrop isn't exactly impulsive."

Marie smiled slightly. "Not impulsive, perhaps. But stubborn."

Mrs. Boardman gave an unladylike grunt. "Just like his father was before him. And just about as closemouthed, too. When I asked him questions about you all he would say was that he knew I'd like you."

"I hope you do."

Mrs. Boardman looked at her sharply and then murmured, "I see no reason why I shouldn't, my dear. But I still haven't the faintest idea how you two met. Not, of course, that it makes any difference...."

Marie hesitated momentarily. It was a question that she knew would be asked many times and in many indirect ways in the days to come.

A simple answer, she had long since decided, would be the best. One with a thin element of the truth.

She said casually, "It was at the home of a friend of mine. Winthrop was one of the guests."

Mrs. Boardman nodded, apparently content. She was a large woman, with the same nervous impatience that characterized her son. She was in the sixties and made no effort to conceal the fact. Her black hair was liberally streaked with gray; she affected plain, common-sense clothes that were almost mannish. She had the forthright bluntness bred by social and financial security.

Formidable, was the word Marie used to herself to define her. And she was reminded for a moment of the strict unyielding manners of Madame Romain....

Winthrop's mother was speaking again.

"I suppose you know there has already been gossip about this marriage. If you don't know, you'll discover it soon enough. The Averys are saying that Helen broke her engagement to Winthrop because of you."

"So?" Marie permitted herself a slight smile. "I do not know this Mlle Avery. But she is a woman so it is logical that she should have her own story to tell."

Once again Mrs. Boardman expressed her feelings with a grunt. "And I imagine Winthrop could tell another story, if he had a mind to. Personally, I never cared too much for either the girl or her mother. Hypocrites, both of them! Maude Avery was a nurse before she married old John, and from what I've heard she slept with every doctor and interne in the hospital. After she led John Avery to the altar you'd think butter wouldn't melt in her mouth, but she was no better than a tramp, if you ask me!"

There was silence for a moment and then Mrs. Boardman said with a laugh, "I hope I didn't shock you, my dear, with an old lady's frankness."

Marie shook her head. Her voice when at last she answered was smoothly even.

"*Mais non.* I was only thinking." She looked up at this strange mother-in-law of hers and smiled mischievously. "Thinking that this Mrs. Avery must be a very practical person. If she had to be a tramp in her younger days, as you say, what better and safer place than in a hospital among doctors."

Mrs. Boardman stared at her blankly for a doubtful minute before bursting into hearty laughter.

"You're all right, my dear. And I have a feeling you'll be able to hold your own in Old Haven no matter what kind of cattishness you run up against."

Marie smiled demurely.

"I hope so," she said softly.

Later that week Mrs. Boardman gave a tea to introduce her daughter-in-law to the local society. At first Marie had been somewhat daunted by the prospect of facing several score of strange women at one time. For not the first time she became keenly conscious of being a foreigner in a foreign land.

She dressed with considerable care, selecting and discarding a half a dozen afternoon frocks before she made her final choice. It was a light silk of misty green, cut along severely simple lines, that fell just below the knee an inch or so longer than the extreme fashion of the period.

When she went down to the drawing room she found Mrs. Boardman superintending the two housemaids in the arrangement of the tea service.

"Could I be of help?"

"There isn't anything to do, my dear. I don't know why I bother making a pretense of serving tea, anyway. All anyone wants these days is a concoction made out of horrible gin and orange juice. The Italian who sells the gin makes it himself, I understand, and the orange juice comes out of cans. But it's very popular."

Marie made a little grimace. "I think I will be unpopular, then, and choose tea."

"With a spot of rum in it," Mrs. Boardman suggested. "I'm happy to say that Winthrop's father had the foresight to stock a considerable cellar long before anybody thought of such a thing as Prohibition." She paused and let her glance sweep over Marie. "You look very smart in that dress, my dear."

Marie eyed her doubtfully. "But not too smart, I hope."

"And why not, for heaven's sake?"

Marie spread out her hands and laughed. "Because I do not wish to appear too chic. It is something that other women resent."

"Let them!" Mrs. Boardman snapped. Then, thinking of resentful women, she remembered something. "I suspect the Averys, mother and daughter, will be here this afternoon. At least, I invited them. Not to have done so would have given them more importance than they rightfully have. You don't mind?"

"But why should I?"

Mrs. Boardman was saved from an immediate answer by the entrance of the first guests. For the next hour Marie's mind was a maze of dimly, sketchily remembered names that she was certain she could never fit to the right faces. She was conscious of numerous eyes covertly and sometimes openly studying her and suddenly was caught up with a feeling of having gone through this same sort of minor ordeal before. It was a moment before she could place it in her mind, and then in a quick flash she remembered. It had been her first day at Madame Gerlaine's when she had sat in the kitchen while the girls in the house came sleepily down to eat. They had watched her then in much the same way, speculating among themselves as to where she had come from and how she managed to be there and exactly how they should behave toward her.

Inwardly she relaxed as she smiled to herself, thinking, After all, the difference was very little. All women were alike in that they distrusted newcomers within their circle, fearing possible competition....

It was at that moment that the girl she had previously identified as Helen Avery spoke to her from halfway across the room.

In a clear voice that cut through the muted hum of conversation she said, "We've all been so anxious to meet you, Marie. And you don't mind if I call you Marie, do you? After all, we've known Winthrop all his life, and it would be a little stuffy to call his wife Mrs. Boardman, don't you think?"

Marie smiled. "I can understand it might be a bit difficult," she said quietly.

She could almost hear the silence that seemed to her imagination to be sweeping the room, and then Helen's voice came again, more loudly and clearly.

"But it was all such a surprise to us. Mother and I were in Paris for the summer, you know, much of the time that Winthrop was there. It seems so strange that we didn't meet you then."

The faintly polite smile stayed on Marie's face. She shrugged her shoulders slightly as though the answer were too obvious to need saying, but that nevertheless she was humoring one who persisted.

"But not at all. I imagine we moved in somewhat different circles." She paused and then added in a tone of gentle explanation, "You see, there is one Paris for the tourists and another for those of us who live there. Naturally the two rarely meet."

She smiled again, as though to soften the implied criticism, and turning her back picked up the threads of an interrupted conversation with a Mrs. Pennyfeather, the head of the local garden club, who was speaking in a strange language that Marie finally discovered with mild amazement was supposed to be French.

She wondered if Helen Avery was fool enough to think she didn't know the story of the broken engagement and the reasons behind it.

CHAPTER TWELVE

THERE WERE TIMES during the course of that first year when Marie wondered about the wisdom of her marriage. In Paris, in the Maison d'Or, the pattern of her life had been orderly and set—she had known exactly what to expect from day to day. And always she had had her plans of the future to which she could look forward.

Now, in a way, the future was at hand. She had a home and security and a husband. There was plenty of money; she had a luxury and an ease of living beyond anything she had ever dared to imagine. Yet at the same time there was something missing.

It was a feeling of permanency, she finally decided. The truth was that a home here didn't seem to mean quite the same thing as it did in France, just as a marriage and the duties of marriage were taken less seriously. The wives of Old Haven spent the better part of their time in a hectic round of social engagements, mostly bridge and dinner parties and dances at the various clubs.

Their homes, seemingly, ran themselves.

Nor did their husbands complain. Apparently they got a vicarious pleasure out of their wives' endless activities; although at times they grumbled and complained about being dragged out of the house to attend some affair they would have been even more disturbed had there been no invitation.

To Marie it seemed a needless form of slavery.

She suggested as much to her husband one night when they were dressing for a dinner dance at the country club. He was cursing mildly as he struggled with putting studs in a stiffbosomed shirt, regretting the necessity of having to dress and go out.

Marie stopped in the process of putting on her stockings.

"Then why do we go, Winthrop?"

He stared at her blankly. "What's that?"

"Why do we go? We could stay home here very nicely, just by ourselves for a change."

Boardman shook his head. "Everyone will be there. It would look odd if we didn't show up."

"But why?"

He frowned at her, frankly puzzled. "I don't follow you."

"Why would it look odd if we didn't appear at the dance?"

"Oh. Well, it's not as though one of us were sick or something like that. We haven't any excuse for not going." Then an idea struck him and he eyed her sharply. "You mean you don't *want* to go?"

She smiled at him. "Of course I want to go, my dear. I only thought that possibly you were too tired...."

He wasn't that tired, he told her gruffly. Besides, there would be plenty of time for staying home when they got too old to do anything else.

He stood watching her for a silent moment as she finished fastening her stockings. Then he said suddenly, "Did I ever tell you that you have damned beautiful legs, Marie?"

She raised an eyebrow. "Only my legs?"

"Beautiful all over," he corrected. His eyes went slowly over her, seemingly noticing for the first time that beneath her open dressing gown she was clad only in brief panties and a narrow lace brassiere. He gave a little laugh. "And I half wish we weren't going out, at that."

Marie waited, wondering if he had changed his mind.

But he hadn't.

He shrugged his shoulders, as though throwing off a thought born of weakness, and said brusquely, "Let's get going, old girl. We're late as it is."

She managed not to sigh audibly.

The parties given in Old Haven always amazed her.

It was difficult to remember that once, in the early days of her marriage, she had been nervous and concerned that she wouldn't know how to behave properly—that she might make some awkward social error in public.

That fear, she discovered soon enough, was needless.

What was more difficult was for her to accustom herself to the general looseness in behavior. Although it was Prohibition, liquor was everywhere in evidence; there was a great deal of excessive drinking in which the women held their own with the men. Along with the general drunkenness went an equal laxity in conversation; the favorite topics and the favorite jokes were ones having to do with sex.

At the country-club dances there were always bets being made as to how many pairs of panties would be found in out-of-the-way nooks in the morning by the club attendants. Then would come the gossip about the girl the summer before who had forgotten that all her undergarments were embroidered with her initials and had never been able to explain what her lace drawers were doing hanging from a clump of bushes by the seventeenth tee.

At that point some woman was always certain to cry out, "They'll never be able to catch me in *that* fix! I play it safe by not wearing any to begin with...."

Marie listened with a bright smile on her face the while she thought of the Maison d'Or. She could imagine the horrified expression on Madame Romain's face if any of the girls in the establishment had behaved in a similar manner. In the first place Madame objected to heavy drinking and to smutty talk. "All our clients are gentlemen," she had been wont to say, "and I trust you girls will remember to act like ladies. If our clients cared for a more vulgar type they would go elsewhere." And her manner always implied that going elsewhere they would not be welcomed back at the Maison d'Or.

But here it was different. Sex not only had the fascination of a forbidden topic, it seemed to influence every social action as well. The men, both young and old, tried to give the impression of being gay libertines, but with a blunt awkwardness that appalled Marie.

The approach, the conversation, was nearly always the same.

"Old Boardman certainly pulled a fast one on us home boys, bringing back a French wife. But you never can tell about these quiet ones...."

"Winthrop is quiet?"

There would be a meaning laugh. "I guess you know the answer to that. But this must seem pretty dull to you after Paris."

"I don't find it so."

"You're just saying that. You French really know how to enjoy yourself and get fun out of life." If they were dancing the man's hand would press against her waist or move over her flank, attempting to draw her closer, as though illustrating how the French got fun out of life and enjoyed themselves. "I was over there a year ago for a couple of weeks. I ran into a Frenchman who showed me the *real* Paris. Not just the Follies and the big nightclubs but the little places down in some cellar where the waitresses came up to your table without a damned stitch on. Man, oh, man! Made me wish I didn't have the wife along!" And the hand would become heavy again with hopeful pressure. "But I guess all that's an old story to you...."

Marie would stiffen her body automatically. "I'm afraid I don't know much about it," she would say evenly. "In France the young girls haven't quite the same liberty that they have here. I really led a very retiring life."

That much, she told herself with a smile, was at least the truth. Neither Madame Romain nor Madame Gerlaine would have permitted any of their girls to run wild at night, visiting the type of tourist resort overrun by streetwalkers.

It would have given the house a bad name.

In their way the women had the same misconception about Paris, the same sexually-tinged reminiscences and avid curiosity. All who had been there seemed to have been impressed by the same things. The chastity belt of former centuries on display at the Cluny Museum. The *bidet* which was a feature of every bathroom. "My dear, when I first saw it I thought it was a foot-bath. But then when George told me what it *really* was I nearly *died* of embarrassment. It was on our honeymoon, too, of all times!"

"How did George know so much?" some one was always sure to ask.

"He claimed a fraternity brother told him. But afterward I *wondered!*"

And they had the usual questions to ask.

"Is it true that they have houses where they put on exhibitions? My husband told me once ..."

"Is it true that the Frenchmen would rather ... ?"

"Is it true... ?"

Marie smiled and looked blank and shrugged "Of such things I cannot say. You know far more than I...."

With constant repetition they came to believe her. Just as they finally believed her at the strictly feminine bridge parties when she insisted that she didn't know any off-color French stories and had never seen any of the famous post cards that supposedly were sold on the sly to tourists on every street corner in Paris.

They believed her, but were frankly puzzled and disappointed. That much she learned one day when inadvertently she overheard several of the younger matrons discussing her one afternoon at a country club tea.

"She dresses smartly enough, I'll admit, but, my God! She's just too damned innocent! You'd think she'd spent all her life in a convent. How that French girl ever snared Winthrop is a mystery to me."

"Maybe she's good in bed."

"I doubt it. She strikes me as too aloof to give a man a really good time. Maybe that's what she needs herself if you come down to it!"

A little bitterly Marie wondered exactly what was expected of her. Of one thing she was quite certain, and that was that she had no intention of changing. She had no desire to go into competition with amateur whores for a dubious social success.

For that was what most of them behaved like, she told herself. Amateurs. Amateurs willing to give themselves for the excitement of the moment and with no thought or plan for the future.

And she thought suddenly of her yellow card, the ticket of her profession that was checked each week by the inspecting doctor and the proper official of the *arrondissement*. She had carried it away with her from the Maison d'Or and now it was safely locked away with her most private papers.

But what would happen if one day she should take it from its hiding place and at one of these gatherings where the talk was purely of men and sex throw the card face up on the table.

If she should say, *"Voila!* If we must behave like whores, let us be honest ones. Here is my card. Where are yours, may I ask?"

At least it would give them something new to talk about....

CHAPTER THIRTEEN

S HE BEGAN TO wonder about Winthrop.

At first she had been a little fearful that in time he would come to regret their marriage, that his mind would begin to dwell on the past before he had met her. But instead he seemed simply to be taking the marriage for granted, much as the other men in the community took their marriages for granted.

He was happiest during the week ends when he could spend his time playing tennis or golf or in the summer sailing his racing sloop on Long Island Sound.

Home was a place to return to when there was nothing else to do.

It had taken time for Marie to fully realize that these habits were due to no fault of her own. They were merely a part of the essential pattern of modern marriage as practiced in Old Haven. Matrimony wasn't supposed to interfere with the hobbies or pleasures or independence of either party. It was a legal license to sleep together and produce children if children happened to be wanted.

Nothing more.

But that wasn't Marie's idea of a full life. She hadn't married Boardman to escape from the Maison d'Or or to live in idle luxury. That much she had made clear from the beginning.

Yet she was honest enough to admit that she couldn't rightfully blame Winthrop for her vague discontent. He had fulfilled his part of the bargain—he had provided her with a comfortable home and social position and security.

It wasn't his fault that the atmosphere into which he had introduced her was essentially a superficial one and one that denied the very thing she wanted most—stability.

And if their marriage was to be a success it was up to her to make it so. Winthrop was too typical of his class to change. He had made one unpredictable gesture when he had broken away from his traditions and training to marry her. It was unlikely that he would ever make another.

Besides, she was too deeply fond of him to want him to ever have regrets.

So now in the same manner that she had once applied herself under Madame Romain's tutelage to acquiring the requisite knowledge and mannerisms of a superior *cocotte* she set about creating a role for herself in Old Haven society. The formula, she discovered soon enough, was a simple one. It merely involved devoting attention to the older women, to working with groups and charity committees that held no attraction for the sportier younger crowd. Even her striking beauty, which normally would have been a liability as far as other women were concerned, became an asset from the fact that she clearly refused to take advantage of it. It wasn't her fault if men chose to make fools of themselves whenever she was about. For it was generally recognized that she gave them no encouragement.

The more elderly matrons of the community nodded approvingly. It all went to prove, they agreed among themselves, that breeding always showed.

Not until they had been married nearly a year did she become pregnant.

Marie was both relieved and delighted by the discovery. Up until that moment she had been somewhat worried, wondering if by chance the years of careful and continuous precautions to prevent conception had in the end left her barren.

She waited another month to be sure before informing Winthrop.

After his first wave of excitement at the news he began making plans for the future.

"If it's a boy I'll register him right away at Groton."

Marie looked mystified. "Groton?"

"The school, you know. He'll go from there right on to Harvard. He'll be with his own crowd from the time he's a youngster and that always makes it easier." He took a turn about the room, busy making mental plans, then stopped short. "When does the doctor say it's due?"

"What doctor?"

He stared at her in shock. "My God! Haven't you seen the doctor yet?"

"But what for? There is nothing wrong that I know."

He was only half listening to her. A moment later he was headed for the telephone in the entrance hall, intent on calling Dr. Marlowe, the family physician, and getting his advice.

Marie looked after him with a puzzled frown and then shrugged her shoulders helplessly. One would think the baby was due any moment instead of some seven months hence. She didn't need a doctor to tell her she was pregnant—nature had already given her a sufficient number of indications. In Laverny such things ran their natural course and when the appointed time came the local midwife aided in the delivery. A doctor was only called in at the last minute in case of serious complications.

Winthrop came back into the room.

"You have an appointment with Marlowe in his office tomorrow at eleven," he announced briskly. "He'll take over and tell you what to do. He's a very good man."

He came over then and stood beside the chair in which she was seated, putting his hand under her chin and raising her head so that he could stare down into her eyes.

"You don't know how happy this makes me, Marie. I guess you know I've been hoping all along for you to give me just this news."

She reached up and patted his hand.

"I'm glad, Winthrop. It makes me very happy, too."

Perhaps children would make a difference, she thought. Perhaps then the house, so carefully designed to give the impression of an English manor house some two centuries old, would lose its stiff newness.

Perhaps then at last it would have the feeling of home—the sort of home of which she had once dreamed in the days when her working world was bound by the four walls of a bedroom.

It would be if she could make it so.

CHAPTER FOURTEEN

S HE CREATED A small scandal by having two children in
quick succession.

The first, Winthrop, Jr., was born in May and the second,
a girl finally christened Alicia, came exactly one year lacking a
week later.

Such haste was considered almost indecent. "The one going
in practically met the other coming out," Helen Avery was
reported to have said. "It's a wonder there wasn't a traffic jam!"

"I thought all French women knew how to take care of
themselves," some one else suggested. "It certainly looks as
though *she* didn't!"

"Maybe she was too lazy. Or perhaps Winthrop wanted it
that way."

"She shouldn't have let him near her so soon afterwards,
anyway. Men never think. If we let them have their way we'd
spend all our lives in bed, either making babies or getting rid
of them!"

Marie heard the rumors and whispers and smiled to herself.
The two pregnancies in rapid sequence had been no accident. She
had known quite well what she was about. Just as she knew of the
existence of other rumors that hadn't as yet reached her.

For Winthrop, left to his own devices during the latter
months of her pregnancy, had followed true to pattern. At home
and in her company he had been attentive and solicitous, with

the guilt-ridden helplessness of a man realizing that he was responsible for a condition that nature had now taken beyond his control.

That had largely marked his attitude during the months preceding the first-born. But during the second pregnancy, succeeding the first so quickly, he became more restless. Marie's enforced inactivity left him at loose ends.

In the beginning she had to make the suggestions that gave him his release.

"Isn't there a dance tonight at the club, Winthrop? Why don't you go?"

"But I don't want to leave you alone."

"I won't be alone. The servants are all here and I'm going to bed early, anyway."

"That wasn't what I meant. It doesn't seem right for me to go out for a good time and leave you at home."

"Don't be ridiculous, darling. Run along and enjoy yourself."

That was in the beginning. Later she didn't have to make the suggestions. He took the lead himself. She became accustomed to hearing him say, "You don't mind if I ..."

And whatever it was she would smile and nod. "Of course I don't mind. It will do you good to get out."

He followed the pattern of prospective fathers in other ways as well. Marriage had accustomed him to a routine sex life and now that it was temporarily interrupted it was more on his mind than in his bachelor days. He was susceptible where previously as a single man he had been wary.

Marie became aware of what was happening when he began telephoning once or twice a week from his offices in Wall Street to announce that some business conference would hold him in town until a late hour. And when, late at night, he did at length return home his explanations were always fulsome and elaborate with detail. But they failed to explain the lingering scent of a strange perfume still clinging to his jacket or the occasional faint smudge of lipstick on his shirt collar.

Marie looked and noted and wisely said nothing.

But then came the business with Celeste which couldn't be overlooked.

Celeste served in the dual role of maid for Marie and nurse for young Winthrop, Junior. She was young, with a small, trim body, jet black hair, and bright, vivacious eyes. She was French Canadian, from a small village near Montreal, and spoke English only imperfectly and with a marked accent. But she was quick and intelligent; she didn't have to be told things twice and went about her work with a cheerful smile.

Marie considered herself fortunate to have found her. It was pleasant having some one around the house who spoke her own language and on whom she could depend.

It never occurred to her that Winthrop would look twice at the girl, not even when friends half jokingly warned her.

"That nursemaid of yours is really much too pretty, Marie. I'm not at all sure I'd want her working for me."

"But why?"

"No need in putting temptation under my husband's nose. God knows men get enough ideas of that kind on their own!"

Marie listened without paying too much attention, thinking only that it was pointless worrying about removing temptations from the path of any man. If such things weren't underfoot they could always be found.

And then one Sunday afternoon she awakened early from a light nap. She turned on the bedside lamp and picked up the novel she had discarded earlier but it failed to hold her interest. It had been a gray, drizzly day but now the rain was coming down heavily, beaten in windy gusts against the windows. Poor

Winthrop, she thought, this was the second Sunday in succession he had been cheated out of his golf.

She wondered idly what he was finding to do to keep himself occupied. Perhaps she should have stayed awake to keep him company.

She swung her legs over the side of the bed and got up carefully, conscious of her increased weight and the awkwardness of her figure. She went into the bathroom and paused long enough in front of the mirror to make sure her appearance was passable. Then she moved on into the adjoining bedroom that Winthrop now occupied.

He wasn't there but she had only half expected he would be. More likely, she thought, he was downstairs in the living room listening to some radio program. Or it might be that friends had dropped in.

In a moment she would go down and see. But now she wanted to speak to Celeste to remind her about a change in the baby's diet.

The girl's room was on the same floor but in the far wing of the house, next to the nursery with its southern exposure. The door, Marie noticed when she reached there, was not quite closed and when she stopped before it she could hear the low murmur of voices and then a quick, excited laugh.

Without conscious thought she pushed open the door.

She stood there silently in the doorway, staring at the bed across the room. Winthrop and Celeste were stretched out there, although the girl was half hidden within his massive embrace. Her thighs were a startling white against the black of her rumpled uniform skirt and the silk of her stocking tops. She was moving and twisting her body in a mockery of resistance while her soft cries of protest ended in gurgling laughter.

"*Mais, m'sieu!* Please … It is dangerous here.…"

It was then that Marie spoke quietly from her place in the doorway.

"*Tu as raison, Celeste.* Such things are always dangerous."

There was a startled gasp and a flurry of bodies on the bed. For a blurred moment Marie could see Winthrop's face gaping at her in consternation.

Then she turned and walked away.

She walked slowly, thoughtfully, until she was in her own room and the door was closed. She went and sat down on the edge of the bed and lit a cigarette, studying the curling spiral of smoke intently as though any minute she could find an answer there to the questions she was asking herself.

She knew what was expected of her; she had heard over and over again the stories of other women who had caught their husbands involved in affairs. Not caught them so openly, perhaps, but sufficiently to make the accusation of infidelity stick. And the outcome was usually the same. If there wasn't a divorce there were the threats of one—threats that were only kept from becoming reality by the abject humility of the guilty husband.

"Believe me, I don't have to worry about *my* husband straying out of bounds!" she had heard more than one wife boast. "He slipped once and he knows what will happen if I ever catch him at it again.…"

But a home held together by threats and recriminations was no home at all. It might be possible to frighten a husband into an outward pattern of domestic faithfulness, but fear could not alone remove desire.

And as long as the unfaithfulness remained purely physical it could be kept in its proper place. It became of emotional importance only if one made it so.

She heard the sound of movement in the adjoining room and a moment later the connecting door opened and Winthrop appeared.

He hesitated on the threshold before entering, almost as though waiting permission. Then when she remained silent he began in a quick rush of words, "Look here, Marie, I want to talk to you. I mean, I want to explain—"

She looked at him curiously. "Explain what?"

"I swear I don't know what got into me. I must have been crazy! I didn't have any intention … I mean, I just went down to the nursery to take a look at the youngster. Celeste was there and we started joking and the next thing I knew—" He broke off with a helpless shrug.

Marie smiled faintly as she concentrated on stubbing out her cigarette in the ash tray. "Don't tell me, Winthrop, that she seduced you."

His face reddened.

"I didn't mean that. It wasn't her fault. It was just—I swear to God I don't know what it was!"

"It seemed quite simple," Marie said softly. "After all, she is an attractive little baggage and you are a man. And it is raining too heavily for you to play golf or even go to the club so you were bored. Such things happen when there is nothing else to do."

He stared at her, his expression confused and worried, plainly trying to crystalize his jumbled thoughts into words.

Marie came to his rescue.

She took a cigarette from the silver box on the bed table and held it up.

"Would you give me a light, please. And I think I should like to go downstairs and sit by the fireplace where it is warm and cheerful and have tea. When it rains like this it reminds me too much of Normandy."

She stood up slowly and started for the bathroom.

Boardman said, "But, look …"

She paused in the doorway.

"Run along and order the tea, Winthrop. That is the most important thing just now."

The bathroom door closed behind her.

But there was still the problem of Celeste.

She found her in her room, dabbing at tear-reddened eyes with a crumpled handkerchief as she went about her packing. She spun about as she heard Marie enter the room and cried out in a frightened voice, "Oh, madame."

Marie ignored her tears. "And just what stupidity are you planning now?"

"Please, madame! I am so ashamed! I never meant to … I don't know how—"

"You don't know how it happened," Marie finished for her tartly. "Naturally. But now you know. It is simply a matter of getting on a bed and assuming a certain position."

Celeste broke out in a fresh burst of tears. "I swear, madame, it was the first time …"

Marie shrugged. It might have been the first time with Winthrop, perhaps, but certainly not with others. She was willing to wager that the girl would have to think far back to recall her virginity. But that was another matter and had nothing to do with the present.

"So now you intend to make matters worse by running away. And what happens to the little one—who is going to look after him?"

Celeste swallowed. "I could stay until you find some one to replace …"

"I don't intend to find anybody to replace you. Stop making more of a tool of yourself than you have already and unpack your things. Wash your eyes with cold water and get in the nursery where you belong." She turned to leave and then paused long enough to toss a final admonition over her shoulder. "And in the future see that you confine your tender activities to the nursery. Is that understood?"

"I promise, madame."

"Nous verrons ce que nous verrons," Marie said warningly. "We shall see...."

During the next few days it became clear that Boardman was at first puzzled and then embarrassed by the continued presence of the nursemaid in the house.

Finally he was unable to keep from speaking about it.

"Are you having trouble finding a new nursemaid?"

Marie looked at him in surprise. "A new nursemaid?" But why should I be looking for one?"

Boardman reddened, plainly regretting that he had brought up the subject.

"Well—I just thought. I mean to say, under the circumstances ..." His words trailed off in confusion.

Marie smiled. "Under the circumstances, my dear, I would only be punishing myself by dismissing Celeste. She understands children, she does her work well, and in the nursery I trust her completely. As for other matters—" She paused and shrugged. "She was not alone, you remember. It still takes two to indulge in such affairs. And dismissing Celeste and replacing her with another would be no assurance the same thing wouldn't happen again. Not unless I replaced her with some ancient crone and I see no reason why I should further punish myself by surrounding myself with ugliness. It is simple, is it not?"

He made no immediate answer. Marie glanced at him quickly and then away, pretending to concentrate on the needlework in her lap. She had a feeling she knew quite well the direction his turbulent thoughts were taking him. He really wanted her to get rid of the girl but he couldn't come right out and say so.

There was no way he could even suggest it without being put in an unpleasant light. After all, the girl had surrendered her body to him—given in to his sudden uncontrollable desire. He couldn't rightfully blame her now for giving him what he had demanded.

Yet the fact that she was still there in the house upset him. It was too constant a reminder of his weakness and guilt. It was a damned sight worse than if Marie had made a violent scene, giving him something tangible against which he could protest.

He said half apologetically, "Well, it's damned decent of you to take such an attitude. Not many women would."

Marie smiled.

"I'm not being decent," she said truthfully. "Merely selfish."

Boardman frowned at her and then shook his head as he gave up trying to understand.

CHAPTER FIFTEEN

A GOOD MANY changes, social as well as material, took place in Old Haven during the depression years. Many of the old estates were closed or put on the market for sale; there was a general reshuffling of habits and customs.

Boardman had been affected by the stock market crash but not as badly as many of his friends.

"Most of my losses were on paper," he explained to Marie. "I've always kept the bulk of the family money in fairly solid stocks and bonds, in companies where we have a finger in the management. But there's next to no trading in the market right now and that means the income from the brokerage office is cut down to nothing. Less than nothing, actually. We're not even making expenses."

Marie glanced up at him. "Do you mean we shall have to give up this house?"

He hesitated. "No. It's not quite as bad as that. Not yet, at any rate. But we'll have to retrench a little. Let some of the servants go, perhaps."

Marie wondered if he were thinking of the nursemaid Celeste who was still with them. Despite the long lapse of time since that rainy afternoon when she had discovered the two of them on the bed together Winthrop was still awkwardly ill at ease in the girl's presence. He treated her with a stiff and cool formality that sought to deny he had ever behaved any other way toward her.

Marie merely smiled inwardly and pretended not to notice.

The thought of domestic retrenchment didn't disturb her. She still had the French peasant's ingrained feeling for economy and horror of waste; more than once she had been appalled at the needless extravagance of entertainment as it was done in Old Haven. At cocktail and dinner parties there was always too much of everything—food was toyed with and nibbled at rather than eaten. All of Laverny could have lived well on what went into the garbage pails of any of a half dozen Old Haven families.

Now she said quietly, "*Eh, bien.* Set a figure for the household allowance and I will see that we live within it."

"And you don't mind?"

"Mind?" She frowned at him for a brief moment and then shrugged lightly. "But why should I mind? We will still continue to live in far more comfort than the majority of people. Is not that enough?"

"You are a remarkable woman, Marie."

"Of that I would not know." She smiled at him across the breakfast table, noting the heavy lines of his face and the uncertainty in his eyes. "I just try to be a good mother and an understanding wife."

She stood up to leave and, passing his chair, rested her hand momentarily on his shoulder in a little gesture of tenderness. Poor Winthrop! He was like so many American men as she had come to understand them. They had no faith in themselves as individuals—take away a fraction of their material possessions and they became unsure of their value, fretted by a feeling of inferiority.

Suddenly Winthrop burst out petulantly, "It's that damned Roosevelt! Once we get him out of the White House things will be different."

"I'm sure they will, *mon cher.*"

It was the following year that the shocking business of the burglar occurred.

Afterward everyone agreed that Marie handled herself extremely well during the frightful affair, not only in courageously facing the burglar himself but in the period of nerve-wracking publicity that followed.

Another woman might have dramatized her role as heroine. Marie, however, insisted on being modestly realistic.

"He was an intruder in the house and I feared for my home and my children. It is natural to protect what is dearest to you."

"But weren't you frightened?" some one always demanded breathlessly. "Weren't you terrified?"

Marie smiled a trifle sadly. "When primitive instincts are aroused there is little time for fear. Now that it is over I feel sorry for the poor, unfortunate man...."

The facts, as luridly detailed in the New York tabloids and rehashed over Old Haven dinner tables, were simple and routine enough.

It happened on a Thursday night when, except for the children, Marie was alone in the house. For on Thursdays, according to immemorial custom, the servants had the day off. As a general rule Winthrop also absented himself on such evenings, remaining in town with the excuse of one of his mysterious business conferences.

Marie had prepared a light dinner for herself and the children, put them to bed an hour later, and then sat by herself in the living room reading and listening to the radio.

It was somewhat after ten when she started upstairs to her bedroom.

As she recounted the affair later to the police officials, it was when she reached her bedroom door that she became aware of the sound of movement inside the room. She hesitated with her hand reaching for the knob, listening carefully to make sure she wasn't just being the victim of nervousness. Then she heard another muted sound that made her certain.

Quietly then she had gone into her husband's room and tiptoed to the bedside table in the drawer of which Winthrop was in the habit of keeping a revolver. With the gun in hand she had moved through the connecting dressing room and surprised the burglar in the act of rifling her jewel case.

Caught in the act, and apparently disdainful of the weapon pointed at him, he had charged at her.

That was when she had fired in self-defense. But she had meant only to wound the man.

Not to kill him.

Of that she was quite insistent. Ralph Blakely, the County District Attorney, was properly sympathetic and understanding.

"Don't let it prey on your mind, Mrs. Boardman," he begged. "The man's death was his own fault, not yours. He took a calculated risk and lost. That's what it comes down to."

Marie nodded sadly. "I suppose you are right, *m'sieu*. As you say, he should not have come here in the first place...."

Winthrop was overly solicitous and attentive throughout the trying time. He was embarrassed by a feeling of guilt that he had left Marie at home alone and at the same time was worried that routine police inquiries might turn up the fact that the business conference that had kept him in town had largely taken place in a small apartment on Central Park West where a former stenographer now took a different kind of private dictation.

He would have been even more upset had he been aware that Marie strongly suspected where he had been and more or less what he had been doing. As it was, he managed to ease his conscience by acting as a buffer between Marie and the reporters and police, protecting her—as he called it—from additional strain.

The story ran longer in the newspapers than it normally would have because of the background of the dead burglar.

Due investigation disclosed that the man had been an amateur. At least, he had no police record that could be uncovered. On the contrary, it was learned that he was a former reporter. He had held a succession of jobs for various American press bureaus in Europe during the 20's but had been fired from most of them for excessive drinking. The same thing had happened when he returned to New York. For the past two years, according to his former friends, Charlie Marvin had eked out a sketchy living writing occasional special feature articles.

As nearly as could be discovered, his attempted burglary of the Boardman home had been his first—as well as last—foray into outright crime.

It was just unfortunate happenstance that had involved Marie Boardman in the unpleasant experience.

That was the official and accepted version. Only two persons ever knew the full and definite truth and one of them only lived with the full knowledge of what was happening for a brief and horror-struck moment.

That one was Charlie Marvin, who became aware of the truth too late, and now his lips were sealed forever.

The other was Marie.

That may have been the reason for her half-sad, half-enigmatic smile whenever Winthrop said with clumsy helpfulness, "The thing for you to do now is forget it all, honey. Just wipe it out of your mind as though it never happened."

"Yes, my dear," she said. "There's nothing else to do, is there?"

But it was a long time before she could forget Charlie Marvin. At night when she was alone, or at odd moments during the day, she would suddenly find herself remembering the first time she had seen him.

That had been several days before the fateful evening.

It was a mild afternoon in mid-May and she had gone to the Country Day School to walk home with the children, a custom she kept whenever possible.

It was an hour of the day to which she looked forward, the one in which she always became more conscious of her pride and happiness in the family she had created. And at the same time it enabled her to keep a watchful, tender eye on the rapidly developing, sharply different personalities of the two.

Winthrop, Jr., was already a small replica of his father in many ways. He was stolid and, in his small way, materialistic, concerned largely with the physical pleasures of the moment and lacking his younger sister Alicia's quiet sensitivity.

On this afternoon he was overly exuberant, constantly interrupting Alicia as she tried to recount some minor happening of the school day.

"Let Alicia finish," Marie told him. "It's not very good manners to interrupt, you know."

"Poof on manners!" said Junior.

Marie regarded him quietly. "And just what do you mean by that, young man?"

"It's what Stinky Davis says. Stinky says his old man says that if you've got plenty of money it don't matter how you act. It's the old money that counts, and not nothing else."

"Not anything else," Marie corrected automatically. Then she added more slowly, "And I'm afraid your friend—ah, Stinky—isn't quite correct. There are a great many things that can't be bought with money."

"Like what?"

Marie thought for a moment and then said gently, "Like you and your sister. Your father and I couldn't have bought you with money."

Young Winthrop was unconvinced. "What did you buy us with, then?"

Once again Marie hesitated.

"Love," she said at last.

Clearly it wasn't an answer that made much sense to Junior. He frowned up at her and then his attention became occupied by a parked car on which a tire was being changed.

It was Alicia who picked up the word.

"What is love, mummy?"

Marie smiled down at her, touching the top of her head lightly with her hand.

"It's what I feel for you and Winnie. It's what I hope you both feel for me."

"Is it what you feel for daddy, too?"

Marie hesitated only a fraction of a minute before she answered with a smile, "Of course it is, my dear. Husbands and wives always love one another."

"Even when they don't live together, like Eunice Taylor's mother and father?"

"Even when they don't live together...."

It was not until they reached home, and were turning up the curving, white-oyster-shell driveway, that she noticed the thin man lurking there.

She had the vague impression that she had seen him before but without really taking note of him. Now, however, she became aware that he was watching her covertly, almost as though he were waiting for her to keep some appointment he had already made in his mind.

It annoyed her and she turned her gaze away to follow the children scampering across the lawn when she heard his voice across the short distance that separated them.

"Mrs. Boardman. Just a moment, Mrs. Boardman."

She paused and glanced over her shoulder at him, saying nothing.

"I want to talk to you, Mrs. Boardman."

She had a curious feeling that there was something odd in the way he pronounced her name, a subtle and deliberate emphasis that was faintly mocking.

She sent another quick, instinctively protective glance after the children and said tersely, "Then talk."

"It isn't a matter to shout about. At least, I imagine you'd prefer that I didn't."

She frowned and with a shrug moved nearer, wondering even as she did so why she bothered.

And at the same time she became aware again of the sharp yet somehow furtive scrutiny of the thin stranger. All at once he was speaking in a quick rush of words and her mind was trying to reject their meaning even as her ears heard the sound.

"I wanted to talk to you about Paris," he was saying. "About Paris and the Maison d'Or. You remember, don't you, Yvonne?"

CHAPTER SIXTEEN

S HE STOOD LOOKING at him.

She saw a thin, middle-aged man with a grayishly gaunt face marked with the tell-tale lines of dissipation. His pale blue eyes were the watery, faintly blood-shot eyes of the heavy drinker; under her steady gaze they shifted nervously between moments of staring at her defiantly. His dark suit was neatly pressed but ill-fitting, and the white shirt he wore had been badly laundered and as badly ironed.

He was the first to break the silence.

"Well, what about it? Don't you think we ought to have a little private talk about Paris and the good old days?"

"I see no reason why we should," Marie said stiffly. "I've never seen you before in my life and I haven't the faintest idea what you are talking about."

"Haven't you?" He gave a short laugh. He pulled a crumpled pack of cigarettes from his pocket and put one in his mouth and lit it. The hand that held the match trembled badly. "I don't think your memory can be that short, *Mrs. Boardman*. Even though you might like it to be."

"I'm afraid you're making a very stupid mistake."

He shook his head with a quick gesture. "Not the kind of a mistake you mean. I know what I'm talking about. I used to go to the Maison d'Or in the old days when I was working on the papers in Paris. That was when I had more money." He stopped and gave his short, rasping laugh again. "That was when everybody had more money. That's when I first saw you—and I never forget a face. I've got one of those funny photographic memories that can recall something exactly, years afterward."

Marie found herself answering mechanically, without conscious thought.

"This time your memory has played you false."

She needn't think he was depending on his memory alone, he told her. "It started me off, that's all. A couple of months ago I spotted a picture of you in the society pages of the *Times* and it rang a bell. So I started digging. Whatever else they say about me they've all got to admit that old Charlie Marvin gets his story once he goes after it. And it's easy enough to have the public records in Paris checked if you have the right contacts. And I've still got friends over there." He paused and looked at her sharply, almost as though he expected her to deny that he had friends, and when she remained silent went on in a slower tone of voice, "So that's the way it is, Yvonne. Or would you rather I called you Marie Courcel, of Laverny?"

"You talk in riddles," Marie told him impatiently. "What is it that you are trying to say?"

He looked at her with a frown and took another quick puff on his cigarette.

"I thought I made myself clear. I'm a newspaperman—that is, I make my money writing special features. And this is a story that can be worth a great deal. It might even get me back on a steady job."

Marie confined herself to one word. "So?"

Charlie Marvin spread his hands out. "So I would be losing considerable if I didn't print it—if I forgot about it. I would be making a financial sacrifice and right now I'm not in a position to do that." His watery eyes sought to become knowing and cynical. "I haven't had your lucky breaks in life, *Mrs. Boardman*."

Marie stood there, her expression carefully blank, her mind trying to grasp what had happened and to put it into order and find some answer. To any onlooker the scene would have seemed no more than the mistress of the house chatting casually with a passing acquaintance. She turned and swept her eyes over the rolling lawns and carefully tended gardens and the solid permanence of the massive house. This was security—security that was now threatened by this unpleasant ruin of a man standing in shaky stubbornness on the other side of the boxwood hedge.

She bent down and picked up a dry twig that marred the neat perfection of the clipped grass. The whole thing was fantastic. It had happened too quickly and without warning.

But such things always happened without warning, she reminded herself.

She straightened up and looked at the man waiting so tensely for her answer.

She said, "I am still confused by your conversation. But at any rate, this is no proper place to talk."

"Where then?"

Today was Tuesday, she thought. And on Thursday the servants would be away, it was their day off. In all likelihood Winthrop wouldn't be home, either. He took advantage of such weekly occasions to remain in town under the guise of being considerate. "You won't have to worry about me for dinner," he usually said. "I'll probably be tied up in town. And you enjoy eating alone with the children."

Charlie Marvin broke in on her thoughts by repeating his question. "Where can we talk, then?"

"The day after tomorrow," she told him. "Come in the evening, around ten o'clock. No one else will be here at that hour."

"No one?"

"That is what I said. The servants will be away and my husband will be in the city. Come then."

Suddenly she wanted no more to say to the man. She turned and walked slowly away across the lawn, leaving the man staring after her in hesitant doubtfulness. If she had remained, she was certain he would have objected to her proposed meeting place and would have suggested some other location and time.

Now it was too late.

She had a great deal to think about during the next forty-eight hours. Almost at once she dismissed from her mind any idea of confiding in Winthrop. His immediate reaction would be to seek the aid of his lawyers. It might be that in the end they could do something to silence Charlie Marvin but she rather doubted it. It was almost inevitable that there would be unpleasant publicity of one sort or another.

Of that she was certain.

Just as she was certain that paying money to Marvin now wouldn't remove him as a future threat. Blackmailers didn't work that way. They were like a secret disease that could only be temporarily assuaged with the opiate of money and once the drug had worn off became again demanding.

That was how it would be with this man Marvin. Even when he was not an immediate problem the mere knowledge of his existence would be enough. It would be too much, really. Far, far too much …

And she thought of the years that had gone by since she had walked out of the doors of the Maison d'Or for the last time. She thought of the children, Winthrop, Jr. and Alicia. The boy was now nearly ten and the girl just a year and a half younger. Both were at the wrong age for any whisper of scandal to taint their lives. If there ever was a right age, that is. But definitely they were too young and impressionable to have their carefully routined lives upset or thrown out of order.

She thought of the solid security of the house that over the years she had managed to transfuse into the warmth of a home and she thought of the position she had created for herself in Old Haven society. The substance of the security she had longed for as a child was now hers, and if Winthrop were neither the perfect lover nor the perfect husband that was of minor importance. One couldn't have everything; one did the best with what one had. It was more sensible to be appreciative of Winthrop's conventionally good qualities and to overlook his shortcomings and weaknesses.

More sensible and less emotionally exhausting.

There were many things to be considered in the light of Charlie Marvin's sudden appearance and demands. Not just what would happen to her, but what would happen to others. And always there remained the problem of what she, herself, should do.

In the end there seemed only one logical answer.

It was exactly one minute after ten when she heard the short, almost tentative ring of the doorbell.

She had been waiting for the sound in the living room but now she allowed a moment to pass before she answered its summons. Then she moved with deliberately unhurried steps through the wide entrance hall, feeling in an odd way as though she were walking through a part that had been rehearsed time and again in her mind but that was now facing the critical judgement of an audience for the first time.

She opened the massive front door and faced Charlie Marvin, blinking at her against the background of darkness. For one brief moment, while he hesitated, her nerves fretted her into impatience.

"Come in," she said hurriedly. *"Mais vite.* Quickly, if you please."

She closed the door behind him as he entered and in the action regained her tight composure. Wordlessly she turned and led the way into the living room. She was wearing a thin negligee of black chiffon that she had chosen with cool intention. She had nothing on under it and was aware that against the light every line of her figure was clearly visible.

She dropped into a chair and glanced up.

"So now you are here, where we can talk in private. What is it, exactly, that you wish?"

His eyes were on her legs, outlined beneath the misty chiffon. Slowly she crossed them, careless of the folds of the negligee slipping aside.

She prompted quietly, "Well?"

"I thought it was understood. I have a story that is worth money and that I want to sell." He hesitated and she could see the constriction of his throat as he swallowed while his eyes remained intent on her body. "It's one you should want to buy yourself."

"But why?"

"You know damned well why!" he burst out. Then with an effort he tried to regain his former air of jaunty cynicism. "I went to the Maison d'Or often enough myself in the old days. But I never had the good fortune to—to …"

His words trailed off as she bent forward to take a cigarette from the rosewood and silver box on a low table by the chair. She seemed quite unconscious that the action exposed in full the creamy perfection of her breasts as she flicked a lighter into flame.

She asked softly, "And what do you think this infamous story of yours might be worth, my friend?"

Again he hesitated, as though having difficulty in bringing his thoughts to bear on the matter at hand. His voice when he answered at last was a hoarse mumble.

"About five thousand dollars."

"You exaggerate! Why should I pay that much for something that may not even interest me?"

He made a quick sweeping gesture with one trembling hand. "It depends on how much all this interests you. Five thousand is very little for a woman in your position."

Marie sighed and stood up, letting the folds of her negligee drape softly back into place over her body. She looked at him sleepily out of the violet shadows of her eyes.

"You are very adamant, *m'sieu*. For the moment it would seem that I can deny you nothing. The money is in my bedroom. Suppose we go there." She paused in the doorway, as though aware for the first time of his hesitancy, and then laughed throatily. "Don't tell me that you are afraid! I told you that all the servants are out. We will be quite alone...."

As he followed her up the stairs, his eyes fascinated by the smooth undulations of the hips moving before him, Charlie Marvin lost for the first time his feeling of nervous uncertainty. Up to that moment he had been none too sure of the course he had chosen to follow. More than once he had been tempted to give the whole idea up and content himself with selling the choice item of scandal to some gossip columnist. But then he reminded himself of the other opportunities he had given up through inertia or laziness in the past and it became a matter of self-discipline to follow the business through.

Yet in his most hopeful dreams he hadn't thought it would be this easy or that there would be the sort of extra dividend that was now being clearly indicated by her invitation to the bedroom.

He was in that bedroom now, glancing at the immaculate neatness of the over-sized bed, wondering a little nervously exactly what his next move should be.

He had to hand it to her, she was calm enough about the whole thing! She hadn't even tried to argue him down on the sum he demanded. She hadn't even made a scene, or become mean and nasty.

On the contrary, she was going to the opposite extreme. Maybe this Winthrop Boardman couldn't satisfy her. Or maybe he, Charlie Marvin, still possessed an attraction for women. Mechanically he passed a hand over his thinning hair and straightened his shoulders a bit.

He heard her saying, "First, I presume, you would like your payment."

"There's no hurry." He laughed with a quick excitement. "As long as you're certain there is no danger of interruption."

"There will be no interruption," she told him calmly. She had crossed the room and was standing by a bureau. There was a jewel case on top and she opened it. "But first I must give you what you came to collect."

She turned to face him but it was a full moment before he realized what she held in her hand as she advanced toward him across the room.

"For God's sake, be careful!" he cried. "What do you think you're doing! You can't—"

The sharp bark of the gun cut him short.

Marie watched him as he half spun about and sagged to the floor. Slowly she walked closer and knelt down beside him, her lips twitching in a little grimace of distaste as she felt for his pulse. His coat jacket was undone and she could see the blood-red stains widening on his shirt front over his heart.

He was dead.

She straightened up wearily and went over to the jewel case on the bureau and selected a diamond and emerald bracelet and two dinner rings. She went back to the body on the floor and slipped the jewelry into a coat pocket.

Then she stood for a long moment with her eyes closed, as though trying to recreate a series of pictures in her mind. The hat! she thought suddenly—he had worn a hat when he arrived.

She went quickly downstairs and found the hat in the entrance hall and returned to drop it on the floor by the head of the body.

She could think of nothing else, except the exhaustion that seemed suddenly to possess her. With a heavy step, and without a backward glance, she went out of the room and down to the telephone to call the police.

There was nothing else she could have done, she told herself dully.

Nothing else....

CHAPTER SEVENTEEN

THE LEGAL QUERIES and routine official procedures were quickly and smoothly completed.

As far as the authorities were concerned, the case of Charles Marvin was closed. But it was another matter with respect to the social gossip of Old Haven. It was a long time before talk died down—talk that was in the main not unkindly but rather speculative and curious.

For weeks after the event Marie was conscious of the veiled glances that followed her in public, just as she was aware of a great deal that was being said even though she could not hear the words themselves.

The role that she was called upon to play was a difficult and a subtle one. Yet she managed to simplify it with the basic logic that was part of her French peasant inheritance. Marvin had been a thief, although not exactly of the type indicated by the circumstances of his death, and as a thief he had threatened her dearest possessions.

For the thief she had no pity. For Marvin as a human being, driven on to his own destruction by weakness and avarice, she had a profound sorrow.

Thus she was truthful when she said with a sigh, as she was called upon so often to say in the days immediately following the shooting, "It is something that I regret very much. If the poor man had only been content to run away rather than threaten me …"

Her words would trail off then, and she would make a small gesture with her hands, silently admitting the futility of such wishful thinking.

It was different with Winthrop.

Once, after he had figured that the shock of the occurrence was over, he said admiringly, "I must say you amazed me, Marie, the way you handled the whole business. Most women would have screamed or gone into hysterics. But you kept a pretty cool head. Hell—I didn't even know you knew how to use a gun."

Marie looked at him silently for a long moment. Then she said slowly and without expression, "Nor did I know, my dear. One never knows what one will do until the circumstances arise."

Winthrop grunted. "Well, you handled it damned well! I couldn't have done better myself."

Another moment passed before Marie said softly, "I wonder...."

He stared at her curiously, frowning uncertainly as he tried to detect an undercurrent of hidden meaning. But Marie was calmly lighting a cigarette, seemingly unaware of his searching scrutiny.

Maybe, he thought belatedly, she doesn't want to talk about it.

Clumsily he changed the subject to the coming dance at the Hunt Club that Saturday night.

CHAPTER EIGHTEEN

A T THIRTY-EIGHT, Marie belied her age by several years. Her figure was still slim and provocative, her face was unlined and her eyes devoid of the heavy shadows of nervous excess that marked so many of the younger matrons of Old Haven.

She managed her household smoothly and efficiently, facing the changing problems of the times with a calm serenity.

Other men envied Boardman his good fortune.

Yet behind the cool façade that Marie presented to the outside world she was constantly on the alert for any new danger that might threaten the private security of her home and her children. She was well enough aware of Winthrop's reputation for philandering and the escapades in which he constantly involved himself. For the most part she dismissed these recurrent affairs with a mental shrug of the shoulders. She was still amazed at the average American woman's adolescent attitude toward sexual fidelity. Fidelity, that is, insofar as the husband was concerned. It was as though by chaining a man to a connubial bed you could somehow chain his wayward thoughts and transient desires as well.

It was a ridiculous warping of values, Marie considered. Marriage was more than a double bed; more than a mechanical mating of two bodies bound together indefinitely by the restricting cords of legality.

She always knew when Winthrop was embarked on a new affair. At such times he always became overly solicitous and awkwardly attentive when he was at home; in his explanations of what kept him in town so often he was explicitly detailed. He gave himself away by his elaborate attempts to act naturally.

Only when the affair of the moment was over did he revert to his normal self, becoming once again typically absent-minded and obtuse, taking his wife and home for granted as part of the accepted pattern of his life.

Once or twice, however, his affairs got out of hand and beyond his control. Then he could no longer pretend to Marie that such things weren't happening.

There was the business of Kay Sargeant, for instance.

Marie first became aware of her by name when she appeared one midmorning in Old Haven.

It was Celeste who announced her, adding, "She says it is about a private and personal matter, of great importance."

With a faint frown Marie considered, wondering for a single weary moment if this was going to be a repetition of the unfortunate Charlie Marvin tragedy. Then she curbed her worry and went down to the living room.

The girl, who had been pacing the floor, turned swiftly at her entrance and began speaking almost at once.

"Perhaps you think it odd of me to come here this way, Mrs. Boardman, but, after all, we are two adult people. I mean, the only really sensible thing to do seemed to be to meet and talk the matter out calmly."

Marie stared at her visitor curiously. She had a feeling that the quick rush of words had been carefully rehearsed but they still meant nothing to her. No more than did this young stranger with her dark hair and dark eyes, dressed in the severe smartness affected by business girls who spoke of their jobs as careers.

"I'm sorry," she said. "I'm afraid I don't quite understand."

"Doesn't my name mean anything to you? Hasn't Winthrop—your husband told you about us?"

Marie shook her head.

"But he must have!" Clearly the girl didn't believe her. "He told me he asked for a divorce but you refused. He told me just last week...."

"Oh!" Marie crossed to a chair and sat down and reached for a cigarette. Almost to herself she murmured, "So you're the one."

"You see?" the girl said accusingly. "He did tell you!"

Once again Marie shook her head. "No, my dear. He didn't tell me anything. But it so happens that I know my husband and—well, shall we say, his weaknesses."

"It's no weakness to fall in love!"

Marie took her time in lighting her cigarette. "Perhaps. Falling in love, as you call it, can be very pleasant. And it is always a convenient excuse for satisfying one's physical cravings." She glanced up at the girl, still pacing the floor, feeling suddenly a little sorry for her. She was so much like all the others of her generation. They felt so secure and modern with their air of bright, brittle sophistication. They faced the world with crisp phrases rather than real knowledge. A primitive woman of the jungles probably had better intuitive judgment in the handling of men. She said gently, "I didn't mean you, of course, my dear. And why don't you sit down and relax. It doesn't help being quite so tense."

Reluctantly Kay Sargeant sat down, sitting upright in a straight-back chair. She declined the cigarette Marie offered. With an attempt to regain her former coolness she said flatly, "So now you know how matters stand. The question is, what are we going to do?"

"Do?" Marie shrugged and spread out her hands. "But why should I do anything? It is not my problem."

"But Winthrop and I love—"

"You said that before, my dear. But there are different kinds of love, as you will learn in time, and some wear themselves out sooner than others. I take it that you once worked or possibly still work for my husband. Yes? Then you certainly knew that he was a married man and you went into your affair with open eyes. You should have known the risks involved." Then a suggestion occurred to her and she looked at the girl more intently. "It may be that one of those risks has already caught up with you. Could it be that you are pregnant?"

Kay Sargeant reddened and snapped angrily, "No! I'm not that old fashioned, thank you. And I wouldn't try to trap a man by any corny line like that!"

"In that case I fail to see why you have come to me." Marie sighed, wondering how she could tell this girl with her shining varnish of self-sufficient lacquer that she had made as much of a fool of herself as any unsophisticated farmer's daughter, yet in the telling not hurt her too much. "You see, my dear, you have been misled, because my husband hasn't been quite truthful. Men never are in such matters. It was easier for him to tell you that he couldn't marry you because I wouldn't give him his freedom than to come out flatly and say he never once considered marriage. Probably he told himself that he was letting you down easily by not being brutally frank. Men are too sentimentally weak when it comes to being honest about their emotions."

Kay Sargeant was listening with an expression of shock on her face. When Marie finished she burst out, "You don't even bother to get upset! You sound as though you were talking about a stranger instead of your own husband. Almost as though you didn't care!"

"I care a great deal," Marie corrected softly. "Perhaps that is why I do not allow myself to become upset over what can't be helped."

She was pensive and thoughtful after Kay Sargeant had left. She was certain that the girl was still unconvinced that her neatly thought-out plans had somehow gone astray, that it wasn't as simple as she had thought to precisely arrange her life in the modern manner.

But she was equally certain that she had been correct in her judgment of Winthrop.

They were dining alone that night and she waited until after dinner, when they were sitting in the living room having coffee and brandy and listening to one of Winthrop's favorite radio programs, before bringing up the subject.

Then it was in answer to one of Winthrop's routine questions about the happenings of the day.

"Nothing at all exciting," she told him. "There was a meeting of the Garden Club at Mrs. Burton's this afternoon, and I went to that, of course." Then she added casually, "And your little friend, Kay Sargeant, was here this morning."

It was a moment before he got the significance of her quiet statement. Then he stopped with his demitasse half raised to his lips and demanded, "What's that, again?"

Marie repeated herself. "Kay Sargeant was here."

"What the hell for?"

Marie glanced at his flushed, angry face and then discreetly away. "She said it was because she was in love with you. Or, to be more correct, that the two of you were in love—and that I was standing in your way."

Boardman reacted with the dramatic fury of the guilty professing innocence.

"She hadn't any right to bother you! The damned little tramp ..."

"Please," Marie cut in. "I wouldn't call her that."

"Well—that's all she is. A hard-boiled little tramp who's sore because she can't have her own way. Hell, she wasn't any trusting virgin to begin with!"

Marie sighed. "It may be so. Still, I would not call her a tramp if I were you. It doesn't speak well for your taste. Let us instead assume that she was a dewy-eyed young innocent who temporarily beguiled you with her charms."

Winthrop stared at his wife, not certain of the degree of sarcasm that might lie behind her words. But her expression was calm, she seemed intent for the moment only on studying the russet-golden reflections of the brandy in the glass she was slowly twirling between her fingers.

He said more loudly than he intended, "Well, what happened?"

"But nothing, actually." Marie shrugged and put her glass down and picked up a cigarette. "The girl told her story and I listened. I don't think she appreciated it when I suggested that she was a trifle naive in her handling of her love life but I was really only trying to help."

There was another question that Winthrop wanted to ask but he found difficulty in putting it into words. If Marie had demanded an explanation he would have found something to say quickly enough. He would have had a cue then on how to behave.

But now there was no clue. Marie's calmly casual attitude left him without the spark needed to flare into impassioned denials. She was acting exactly as she had done that time she caught him with Celeste.

As though it didn't matter ...

Almost angrily he burst out, "Don't you *want* to hear the truth?"

She smiled at him softly through a faint wisp of cigarette smoke. "Perhaps I already know the truth. You had an affair with this girl and you tired of it. It may be that it became too complicated or she became too demanding. No matter—it is over now. That is all that is important, isn't it? That it is over and our home is still here."

Relieved, but with the oddly frustrated feeling of having missed something, Boardman said, "Of course you're right. But none the less, that damned girl was lying!"

Marie closed her eyes, trying without success not to think of Charlie Marvin. Winthrop took so much for granted.

He would never realize all that it cost to protect the security of a home....

CHAPTER NINETEEN

WARENESS OF Winthrop's periodic unfaithfulness made her wonder at times at her own behavior. That his affairs were public knowledge had been brought home to her more than once. And she knew that there was considerable speculation as to her own feelings in the matter.

Some wondered why she put up with it.

Others, more cynically worldly in their remarks, wondered why she did not go and do likewise.

There were times when she was tempted.

She realized, at such moments of longing, that she had missed a great deal in life. An expert at sex, she had never known true passion. She had never been seduced by the soft words of love nor had her senses set on fire by the burning caresses of a lover who for a little space of fragile time was not a man but a god bringing the priceless gift of exquisite ecstasy.

Love of that nature was just a word—a word encountered in romantic novels and plays. There had been no place for it in her youth, either in the brothel of Mme Gerlaine or the Maison d'Or. Then it had been no more than a practiced parody of passion and she had moved from that synthetic *milieu* directly to a matrimonial bed where only connubial acquiescence was required.

Never had her own emotions been brought into play.

There had been opportunities. Casual affairs were the rule rather than the exception in Old Haven, almost a part of the accepted social pattern. At every club dance and dinner a half dozen new flirtations were openly started and as many old ones openly continued. But it was all pretense, Marie thought; the same sort of imitation of the real thing in which she had once been skilled. There was a difference, however ... what she had done for profit and to provide pleasure for paying customers these women did because of an inner need for self-deception. They took on lovers for the same reason they patronized certain dress shops or had their homes periodically redecorated or read the season's most discussed books. It was the smart and sophisticated thing to do. It assured them that they weren't in a rut, that life wasn't passing them by. Just as the men were reassured as to their masculine virility—a quality they always seemed to doubt even when it was being brought into actual operation.

In all the while she had been in Old Haven she had met only one man who definitely attracted her, of whom she thought in moments when her mind should have been elsewhere.

He was Russell Garland, the vice-president of an advertising firm owned by his father-in-law. He was a little better than medium height and angularly thin, with a wide, friendly smile in startling contrast to the normal thoughtfulness of his expression. He did not say a great deal, but when his wife was present he rarely had a chance. Susan Garland was a possessive, overly vivacious little woman, with an endless prattle that was as permanently a part of her as the meticulous waves in her superficially blonde hair.

Whatever her husband said she contradicted or added to or simply took over as a conversational subject for herself. And when that happened Garland would just smile patiently and let her have her way.

Marie felt a certain bond of sympathy for him. Even before she heard the gossip confirming it she had the idea that he was an outsider like herself.

Once, early in their acquaintanceship, he revealed a portion of the truth to her.

It was at a Yacht Club party and they were momentarily alone at their table. She was in the fifth month of her second pregnancy and when he asked her to dance she had declined, pleading weariness.

He had understood and sat down beside her.

"I had much rather talk to you, anyway," he told her. "I've been looking forward to the chance for a long time."

She looked at him curiously. "So?"

He nodded and gave her a quick, half-rueful smile. "Or perhaps it would be more correct to say I just wanted a chance to remember." He spoke now in an easy and almost accentless French. "Do you know Normandy at all?"

Marie hesitated, fighting to keep her face and her voice without expression. Trying not to remember Normandy and Laverny. Trying not to think what this man sitting next to her might be going to ask next.

"A little bit," she said carefully at last. "Why do you ask?"

"Because it is so difficult to explain Normandy to some one who doesn't know it. I spent the happiest summers of my youth there, painting. That was when I had romantic, impractical dreams of someday being a famous artist."

"And what happened to those dreams?"

Garland laughed, a brief sound shockingly without mirth, and tossed off the rest of the highball he was holding in his hand. "What always happens to dreams? I used to work in advertising agencies in the winter, saving up money for each long summer. And then one day I fell in love and had to become practical." He stopped a passing waiter and indicated his empty glass and then laughed again. "Did you realize that I am a very practical man, Mme Boardman?"

He was also a very unhappy man who had had too much to drink, Marie told herself. Enough, at any rate, to reveal more than might be discreet.

She said softly, "There is nothing wrong in practicality. We French, as you know, have a reputation for being a very practical people."

"But of a different sort. Your people have a better sense of values." Involuntarily his eyes swept over the dancing couples until they found his wife. "Here we don't know much about values. We merely discover when it's too late that we've paid too high a price for something that doesn't wear well."

Marie decided it was time the conversation was steered into safer channels. Fortunately at that moment the music stopped; people began drifting back to the table and the talk became general.

But from that night there was an unacknowledged understanding between them. It was nebulous and intangible and never put into words. Neither ever referred to that first conversation, when Garland had so impulsively and imprudently voiced his discontent. Yet the memory remained between them.

So as time went on it was the words that were unspoken rather than spoken that seemed to link them closer. Often, at some party, Marie would glance up to find him looking at her from across the room. For a fleeting moment their eyes would meet and hold, as though each were saying soundlessly, "What are we two doing here? This isn't our life.... We don't belong...

That was true, Marie thought. But it was Garland she felt sorry for, and not herself. He had been trapped by what he once thought was love—and then disillusioned by reality. She remembered his bitter insistence that first time they talked that he was now a practical man. That was the trouble. He was not practical at all. He was a dreamer who could no longer afford the luxury of dreams.

With herself it was different. She had married with her eyes open, unswayed by any romantic promptings of her heart. For her marriage was a career, just as her earlier life in Mme Gerlaine's and the Maison d'Or had been a career.

She had made good her escape from everything she had hated and resented in her childhood.

She smiled at the odd twist of irony that made Russell Garland long with an almost visibly aching nostalgia for the Normandy he had once known. For him it was everything.

For her exactly nothing.

That wasn't quite correct, either, she reminded herself. Normandy, with all the sordid poverty she had known there, *had* provided something. It had been the spur that sent her out in the world to seek a new and different life.

Had she been born elsewhere and under different circumstances everything would have been otherwise.

She would never have been here in Old Haven.

So now, in their occasional moments of carefully casual conversation, whenever Garland spoke of Normandy she often wondered if they were talking of the same place. For he spoke of the shimmering greens of cypress and willow trees reflected in the placid waters of the winding Seine and the translucent shadows of the ancient bridges arching the river at Vernon and the rolling orchards colorful with apple blossoms. And Marie thought, This is not the Normandy I know too well, my friend! You should speak instead of the thick mud miring the roads in the heavy rains of fall and the bleak snows of winter and the ignorance of clumsy peasants sotted with raw Calvados. Of days of drudgery and nights of despair ...

Instead she said softly, "I know very little of Normandy. Perhaps some day I shall be able to see these things you speak about."

"I wish I could be your guide," he allowed himself to say.

She smiled and said nothing.

It was a strange relationship that developed between them— an understanding that needed neither words nor physical nearness to make itself poignantly felt.

Only once did it threaten to become more intimate.

That was on a summer night when there had been a garden party at the Country Club, an annual charity affair given for the benefit of the local Child Welfare Society. Winthrop was there, drinking more heavily than usual and making a fool of himself over some little southern girl who was a guest of the Pearson's.

Marie became increasingly bored and weary of the strain of pretending to ignore what was going on. Unobtrusively she slipped away from the central, brightly lighted group of tables surrounding the temporary dance platform and found her way to shadowy privacy of an arbor at the far edge of the lawn.

It was only when she paused to light a cigarette that she became aware of another figure standing there in the semidarkness.

Then a voice spoke and she recognized him as Russell Garland.

"Are you seeking the same thing as I am, Marie?"

"And what is that?"

"Just an illusion for a moment that the things that are happening around us aren't really so—or if they are so, that then they don't matter."

She hesitated, avoiding a direct answer. Then she said with a little laugh, "At the moment I am seeking only a light for my cigarette."

As he flicked his lighter into flame and held it out their fingertips touched. It was that touch of their hands and the meeting of their eyes over the wavering yellow flame that broke down the barriers so carefuly, so deliberately maintained through the years. There was a fragile, infinitesimal space of time that was endless during which both hesitated against the inevitable. Then his arms were about her and he had drawn her close—so close that in the darkness their bodies were a single silhouette outlined against the blue-blackness of the night. His lips brushed her cheek and his words were a soft whisper against her ear.

"My dear, I've waited so long, so very long for this moment...."

Their lips came together, clinging in the tenderness of a kiss that was not so much a kiss as the wordless expression of a hungry yearning that had gone too long unspoken.

For a moment Marie surrendered herself, letting her heart and her desires and her longing take full possession. Then slowly she withdrew. The tips of her fingers brushed lightly over his lips, shutting off further kisses, as she arched backward against the tight encirclement of his arm.

She said softly, *"Mais non, mon cher. C'est pas posible."*

Reluctantly he half released her.

"We have a right, Marie! We have a right to a little happiness of our own." He attempted to draw her closer again but she evaded him. "We owe nothing to the others!"

She smiled a little sadly in the darkness. "Perhaps not, my dear. But we owe something to ourselves—and to our own dreams."

"But sometimes dreams aren't enough."

Again she smiled sadly.

"But they are safer than reality, my dear. Safer, and far more lasting."

Yet all the while her heart was whispering to her, Perhaps this is it! Perhaps this is the one and the only chance I will ever have to truly know what love really is—to know the exquisite pain that comes from a happiness almost too poignantly sensitive to bear. And it may be that in time to come, in the moments of empty loneliness that are inevitable, I will bitterly regret this perhaps needless gesture of rejection. But all my life I have been honest. I was honest in the practice of my profession at Mme Germaine's and in the Maison d'Or, giving value for payment received. And I can be no less honest now in my role as Winthrop Boardman's wife.

I can't allow myself to behave like these society tramps of Old Haven.

It would be without dignity.

Cheap.

CHAPTER TWENTY

ELEN AVERY WAS still very much on the scene.

She had two marriages and two divorces to her credit, along with a speculative number of highly publicized affairs. She was still an athlete, excelling at golf and tennis and riding, and as a result had kept her slimness. But it was not quite the sleek slimness of her youth; it was more of a gaunt, nervous leanness that was accentuated by the hectic gaiety of her manner. She was deliberately brusque in her speech and actions, openly contemptuous of conventions.

She drank and played hard.

Her first husband had been a customers' man in Wall Street who had gone down with the 1929 crash and out of her life just three months later. When she married again it had been to a boy seven years her junior, the son of wealthy ranchers in Texas of whom no one had ever heard in Old Haven. That had lasted less than two years and had ended in some sort of a scandal in Mexico involving a famous bullfighter, although the gossip as to the exact details was always a little confused and contradictory.

After that she settled down in a small apartment in New York, where over the years she dabbled in a variety of careers, ranging from real estate to social representative for interior decorating firms.

She made periodic visits back to Old Haven.

Inevitably she encountered Winthrop Boardman.

In the beginning such meetings were accidental, the natural result of both moving in the same circles and having the same friends and interests. But in time they became deliberately contrived on Helen Avery's part.

She had watched the course of his marriage with the sharply appraising eye of an experienced poacher. That the marriage had held together and survived as it had she knew was due almost entirely to Marie Boardman.

Winthrop's French wife continued to mystify and puzzle her. She had never been able to rid herself of the feeling that there had been something strange about the marriage. For one thing, it had been too precipitate and Winthrop had never been one to rush headlong into things. And she had never been able to understand how it was that she had had no inkling of Marie's existence up to the time of that marriage; she was certain that she had then known all of Winthrop's friends and associates. Nor had inquiries she had later made among her French friends shed any light on the subject.

None of them had ever heard of anyone named Marie Courcel.

In the beginning she had half suspected—and half wished— that Winthrop had fallen into the hands of a clever adventuress and that in due time the marriage would end in a divorce involving a sizable alimony. It would be no more than he deserved, she told herself privately.

But as the years went on and the marriage continued to hold together despite Winthrop's notorious unfaithfulness she was forced to change her ideas. In all honesty she had to admit that Marie Boardman was an exceptional woman and to all outward appearances was an excellent and conscientious wife. Yet Helen Avery was a little tired of hearing the French woman's praises sung by the matrons of Old Haven.

Although she had nothing on which to base them, she still entertained her private doubts and suspicions.

It was Helen Avery who knowingly brought about the first opportunity for an affair.

She did it adroitly and in a seemingly natural manner.

As her mother had previously done, she made a point of calling on Winthrop for financial advice although by this time such advice could have little practical use. The remnants of the Avery fortune had long since gone; her mother was living meagerly in a genteel boarding house in Old Haven on the slim income provided by a small annuity.

Helen herself was constantly in debt.

It was after her third visit to his office that she called him late one afternoon and suggested he stop by her apartment on his way to the Grand Central.

"I haven't time to get downtown before you leave," she explained casually. "And after all you haven't seen my new place yet. It won't take you out of your way, either. It's on Lexington, just three blocks from the station."

Boardman was of two minds about it, but could find no quick reason to refuse the invitation. Particularly when Helen added, "It's rather important that I see you, Winnie."

She had drinks waiting for him and was attired in a semi-tailored lounging robe that displayed most of her legs when she crossed them.

The apartment itself both depressed Winthrop and made him feel slightly ill at ease. It was clearly just one room with a bath and diminutive kitchenette. The vanity table with its jars and pots of rouge and pomades, the studio couch heaped with pillows and the stockings draped carelessly over a chair back, gave it all the intimacy of a bedroom.

He sat nursing his highball, seeking for the right thing to say.

"You've fixed yourself up very nicely here, Helen."

Her laugh had a bitter touch of mockery.

"Don't try to be polite, Winthrop. It's a dreary, middle-class hovel and you know it." She took a quick turn about the room and then added, "A far cry from the old days and the Avery place, isn't it?"

He was conscious of an oddly guilty feeling, as though he were somehow to blame for the circumstances in which she now found herself.

"Well, there have been a lot of changes for all of us."

"Really! That *is* a brilliant observation, Winthrop. Did you make it all by yourself?"

He flushed under her sarcasm.

"Damn it all, Helen! You know what I mean."

"Possibly I know only too well." Suddenly her manner changed and she flung herself down on the couch. "I didn't mean to take my moodiness out on you. But this kind of thing gets me down." She paused and gave Boardman a quick, veiled glance and added softly, "Particularly when I let myself think how things could have been if I hadn't been such a fool."

Boardman glanced at her uncomfortably and then away. He felt that she was waiting for him to pick up her cue but he was damned if he could think of anything to say.

The silence was becoming awkward when she spoke again.

"Perhaps we were both a little hasty and foolish, Winthrop...."

He swallowed the final third of his highball in a single gulp. He found his voice.

"I wouldn't say that exactly."

"Why? Because it isn't true—or because you don't quite dare to say it?"

"Don't be ridiculous. Why shouldn't I dare say anything I want to?" In his irritation he slammed his empty glass down on the coffee table more heavily than he intended. "I don't know what the hell you're talking about, anyway. I'm perfectly contented with my life as it is."

She didn't answer in words. Instead her lips twisted slightly in a faintly mocking smile. Once again Boardman felt on the defensive.

He burst out, "Goddamn it, I mean what I say. I *am* perfectly contented."

Helen's smile widened. "But of course you are, Winnie darling. I'm certain we understand one another completely on that score."

Boardman wasn't so certain.

He was even less certain as time went on. It had been too easy to drift into a liaison with Helen—far easier than it was to break it off.

The fact that within a short time she owed him money only complicated matters more. The sums that she borrowed at frequent intervals to meet some pressing bill Boardman immediately dismissed from his mind. Or rather, he tried to dismiss the business. He knew well enough that she would never pay him back but it didn't matter.

He could well afford the gesture.

However, the fact of her indebtedness automatically placed their relationship on a different, more difficult plane. Boardman always felt in the wrong when he tried to refuse one of her requests to stop in the apartment on his way home. Even when his reason for refusing was legitimate he had the nagging feeling in the back of his mind that she might misunderstand and think that he was avoiding her for fear that she would ask for more money.

At such times he wished he could simply give her one sizable check, as he had once given her mother, and thus wipe the slate clean.

But somehow he could never bring himself to do it. It was easier to postpone the final break.

Yet he found himself becoming increasingly annoyed and irritated when he was with her. She had a genius for turning the simplest situation into an occasion for barbed comment.

Sometimes she suggested that Boardman meet her at some popular cocktail lounge or restaurant and when he hesitated she always took quick advantage.

"What's the matter, Winthrop? Are you afraid that some one will see us?"

"There's no need in asking for gossip."

"Gossip? Why should there be gossip because two old friends meet by chance for a drink or dinner?"

He would mutter something then about her knowing damned well that it wasn't by chance and remind her that because of the past they only needed to be seen once together to start all kinds of rumors flying.

Then she would give her slightly bitter, slightly mocking laugh that was beginning to get on his nerves.

"Thank God I haven't a jealous mate of whom I have to live in fear."

"Don't talk like a fool! Marie hasn't a jealous bone in her body."

"You mean that she doesn't care, Winthrop? Is that what you are saying?"

He snorted angrily. "For God's sake, stop twisting everything around!"

And then came the night when in his impatient anger he said one word too many.

He was tired and on edge and had had too much to drink, a habit that he was falling into with increasing frequency. On top of everything he was exasperated with himself and his own weakness in not having broken off with Helen before.

He was still ridden by a sense of guilt.

This night her waspish tongue and her obvious feeling of surety that she could have him whenever she wished at her beck and call provided the final spark to his anger.

She had said, as she had said a hundred times before, "Why do you have to hurry home, darling? Stay here with me." And then she had drawled casually, "At least I am human in bed, not like that French girl."

He glared at her. "Just what the hell do you mean by that?"

"You should know, my pet. Your wife may be a charming hostess and a perfect mother but the betting has always been that she's as sexless and unexciting as a dead fish in bed." She laughed again and ran her hands provocatively over her bare hips. "Could that be the reason you come to see me so often, Winnie, my darling?"

"I come here because I'm a damned fool!"

"Why, Winnie!" Her voice was underlined with mock chagrin. "Is that any way to talk to your substitute wife?"

"Don't talk rot!" He found himself yelling at her in his hot anger. "Thank God I never did marry you. You'd make a farce and a hell of any marriage. A tramp has more sense of decency and faithfulness than you have!"

There was a flat silence and then she said slowly, "What was that you said, Winthrop?"

"You heard me. Compared to you a tramp would be a perfect wife."

Again there was the sharp break of silence. Then, very softly, she asked, "And just how do you know that, Winthrop?"

He had made the mistake of saying too much at the wrong time. Now he made the second mistake of remaining silent when he should have spoken.

Helen asked more crisply, "Can't you find a simple answer to a simple question, Winthrop? Or is it that you don't want to answer?"

"I haven't any more time for your damned nonsense!" Boardman snapped then. "I'm getting the hell out of here."

Helen Avery merely smiled.

For once she was not sorry to see Boardman go. Her mind was busily engaged elsewhere. Long smoldering suspicion and an intuition suddenly sharpened to supersensitivity had at last given her a clue—a clue that she now intended following with all the tenacity born of hatred and envy.

It had taken a long time but now she was somehow certain of the end.

CHAPTER TWENTY-ONE

I T TOOK NEARLY ten weeks for Helen Avery to gather together the information she sought.

It was a tedious and expensive process, involving the hiring of a firm of private investigators in Paris. She borrowed the money from Boardman and it provided her a sardonic satisfaction whenever she reminded herself that he was actually, even if unknowingly, footing the bills for his own downfall.

The trail began when the records of the marriage were finally unearthed in the municipal archives in Paris. It led then to Laverny and the bleakly depressing poverty of the Courcel farm.

And there, for a week or two, the trail ended, seemingly vanishing into thin air as the girl then known as Marie Courcel had herself once vanished.

It took the running down of a dozen bits of nebulous gossip and half-forgotten rumors to pick up the trail again and arrive, figuratively speaking, at the long since closed doors of Madame Gerlaine's just off the rue Blondel.

After that things moved more swiftly.

It was merely a matter of discreetly checking the records of that branch of the Health Department that concerned itself with the registration and inspection of prostitutes, both streetwalkers and the inmates of accredited houses.

The next and final step was to the ornate portals of the Maison d'Or.

And now, as she studied the accumulated reports, Helen Avery began remembering odd bits from that early summer in Paris when her engagement to Boardman had been so abruptly broken. At the time she had been concerned only with her own role in the break-up, and her wilfully stupid indiscretions that had brought it about.

That Boardman might seek solace elsewhere hadn't occurred to her then and she had been arrogantly sure that somehow or other she could patch things up in due season.

His marriage, with the attendant revelation that he had a private life and friends in Paris of whom she knew nothing, had been a shock.

But now it all fell into a pattern. She recalled as though it were only yesterday his vague explanations and shallow evasions the following day after he had spent an evening of doing the town with fraternity brothers. Ted Stover had been one, she remembered, and Larry Brewster another. She hadn't cared then—in fact she had hoped that Boardman was having a final bachelor fling so that she could justify to herself her own behavior.

Her feminine vanity had been bitterly wounded by her failure to seduce Winthrop into a premarital affair. In self-defense she had told herself that it was because of his ingrained stuffiness.

Now she was certain that there had been another more worldly and logical reason.

At the very moment he was accusing her of shamelessness he himself was undoubtedly involved in his affair with Marie.

The affair that led to the marriage she had never been able to understand up until now.

CHAPTER TWENTY-TWO

NEVITABLY, MARIE HAD been aware of the changes in Winthrop's moods. At times he was nervous and absent-minded and at other times overly attentive.

From long experience Marie recognized the symptoms.

She had already heard rumors that Winthrop and Helen Avery were being seen together in town. Somehow she wasn't particularly disturbed, partly because by now she had grown philosophically accustomed to Winthrop's affairs and partly because she couldn't bring herself to believe that Helen Avery could hold his attention for long.

So she had no premonition of impending danger on the afternoon he returned home earlier than usual and more worried and distraught than she had ever seen him.

But she was faintly puzzled by the somberness of his tone when he spoke.

That was when he led the way into the library that he used as a den and closed the door carefully.

"I have to talk to you seriously, Marie. It's about something—well, it's pretty bad." He took a half turn about the room and paused. "I'm afraid it's going to be a bad shock, my dear."

She gave him a patient smile.

"I don't think anything would shock me greatly, Winthrop. Is it about another affair that you wish to tell me?"

He avoided her eyes.

"In a way. But this time it is something worse—something from which there seems no escape."

She looked at him curiously.

"Are you trying to tell me that you are in love with some one else?"

"Good God, no! I've been a fool, but more of a fool than ever before. I swear to God I don't know what I did to give her the idea in the first place. I must have said the wrong thing at the wrong time. I remember I was drinking and I was angry and I flared up and called her names. And I was right! She's nothing but a cheap, blackmailing tramp!"

It was then that Marie felt the first inner quiver of apprehension and fear.

She said quietly, "Suppose you start in at the beginning, Winthrop. I have an idea that you are talking about Helen Avery but I still don't quite understand."

But he had difficulty in telling the story coherently, for at the same time he was trying to explain what had happened he was seeking for excuses for his own role in the affair.

"… and somehow she suspected something," he finished at last. "She got hold of some detective outfit or other in Paris. She showed me copies of all their reports. She knows everything—*every damned thing about us!*"

"Everything?" Marie asked softly. "I wonder …"

Boardman swore in frustrated anger. "Everything, I tell you. And as though that wasn't bad enough, she's even making up things."

"What sort of things?"

"About that burglary business that happened. Charlie whatever-his-name-was that you caught stealing your jewels. She's saying now that there was something fishy about that. *I* know damned well there wasn't and so does everyone else, but that won't stop her making a stink about it. Along with everything else!"

Marie closed her eyes to keep her own inner feelings masked. She thought of Charlie Marvin and the way he had looked when he saw her holding the gun pointed at him. The way he had cried out in sudden desperate alarm, "For God's sake be careful! You can't ..."

And the way his words had been choked off by the sharp, flat report of the gun.

And now, through Winthrop's stupidity, there was another blackmailer threatening the security of her home—threatening the happiness and future of her children.

She asked tonelessly, "Just what do you intend to do, Winthrop?"

"I can pay her off, I suppose. She's money-hungry, just like her mother. It will be expensive but worth it! Maybe if I guarantee her an income of so much a year as long as she keeps her mouth shut, she'll be satisfied."

Marie found herself shaking her head without quite realizing it.

"No, Winthrop. It won't work. You can never depend on her to keep quiet just for money."

"What the hell else can I do?"

She didn't answer immediately. She felt exhausted and tired, yet her mind was busy going over the past. Going back to Laverny and her early days in Paris. Going back over the years during which she had built up her home and position in Old Haven—the years in which she had denied her own passions and desires for a more lasting security.

The years of decency and honesty and patient understanding of her husband's weaknesses that now seemed to have gone for naught.

One thing was certain—she could not go on living in constant fear of exposure and scandal. For herself she didn't care; she could always return to France and the anonymity of a life in some small village.

But that was not what she had worked and sacrificed so long for. That would leave her children at the mercy of salacious and evil tongues. If that sort of material comfort were all she desired she could have had it long since.

She realized then what she had never before considered. Her roots were no longer in France. Actually, she supposed, she had torn them up when she ran away from Laverny, and her life in Paris, in the brothels of Madame Gerlaine and the Maison d'Or, had by its very nature been as transitory as the illusion of love that had been her stock in trade.

Her roots were here in Old Haven, where her children had been conceived and born and properly raised. Here where over a decade and a half she had transformed the once characterless structure of stone and wood into the warmth of a home.

Here where she was known and accepted.

She said quietly, "There's really only one safe way out, Winthrop."

He looked at her with sudden hope.

"What's that."

"Marry her."

He stared at her as though he couldn't quite believe his ears.

"Good God! Do you know what you're saying?"

"I think I do. That's all Helen Avery has ever wanted, Winthrop. You should know that. She didn't go to all the trouble of finding out about us—about me—just to squeeze money from you. Her one desire is to break up a marriage that she has always resented. And as long as we are married she'll always resent it and hate it. She'll hurt and ruin you just for the sake of hurting me."

"But—"

She raised a hand to stop whatever protest he might be about to make.

"If you marry her it will be simple. She'll have what she wants, has always wanted, then. She'll be happy that at last she has taken you from me."

Boardman could contain himself no longer.

"Goddamn it, I don't want to marry her! I hate her guts, I tell you. I don't want to leave you." He stopped and swallowed and went on in a lower tone. "I know I haven't always acted that way. I've been a fool plenty of times and you've always overlooked it. Maybe you overlooked it too often than was good for me. But I've always known that you were here at home waiting for me." He stopped again and flung his hand out in a sweeping gesture. "Do you think I want anyone else here? Do you think I want the kids calling a woman like Helen 'mother'?"

Marie kept her own voice calm.

"But I have no intention of leaving here, Winthrop. And I most certainly have even less intention of losing custody of the children. I merely said you should marry Helen."

"You're crazy! You don't know what you're asking!"

She smiled without mirth.

"I know quite well what I'm asking, Winthrop. I'm asking you to have the manhood to pay for your own mistakes for once. You were the one who brought this about. Now you should have the decency to protect your family and your reputation and your children.

"And please don't talk to me about sacrifices. About such things I know too much already. I have been making them for fifteen long years because to me a home and children are the most important thing in the world. Because I once made a bargain and I have never been a cheat. I was an honest woman when you met me, and I have been an honest wife. It was stupid, perhaps, but I thought it worth it. I still think so!"

She hesitated, and then with a briefly bitter laugh repeated, "Sacrifices? You don't even know the meaning of the word, my husband. Suppose I should tell you that Helen Avery isn't so far wrong when she questions the details of Charlie Marvin's death?"

Boardman stared at her in blank horror.

"Don't be insane, Marie!"

"I'm not, I assure you. But you might remember that some women will do anything to protect their home. You might keep on remembering it all through the years ahead of you while you are wondering where your wife Helen is and with whom she is sleeping and why you threw away everything because you mistook the provocative movements of a woman's body for passion, or whatever you American men call it. You trick yourselves into believing you are somehow being less like animals in having cheap affairs with any woman willing to fall into bed with them rather than visiting a reputable house. You love to fool yourselves."

"Damn it all, Marie! There must be some other way. You just can't be serious!"

Marie smiled wearily.

"I'm always serious, my dear. A Frenchwoman is never otherwise about the things that matter...."

It was at that moment that Helen Avery was announced.

CHAPTER TWENTY-THREE

I T WAS WINTHROP who was the most upset of the three.

"Goddamn it, Helen!" he stormed. "You might at least have had the decency to stay away!"

Helen gave a brittle laugh.

"I wasn't quite sure of your courage, darling. I wanted to make certain that you fully explained matters to your so properly correct wife."

"I explained. Now get out!"

Marie spoke up softly, "Don't be so rude, Winthrop. After all, why shouldn't Helen be here to discuss your future together?"

"I still have something to say about that!"

Marie looked at him calmly. "As I said before, I'm afraid it is too late for you to have any choice in the matter." She turned then to Helen Avery. "I imagine it will be no surprise if I tell you that Winthrop and I are being divorced and that then he will marry you. That is what you really want, isn't it?"

For a moment Helen was at a loss. "I haven't said so—"

"Under the circumstances you don't need to. Although, to be perfectly frank, I can't say that I envy either of you."

Helen Avery flushed angrily. "If it does happen at least Winthrop won't have to live in fear of people learning that he's married to a tramp!"

"Shut up!" Boardman yelled. "Shut your damned filthy mouth, Helen!"

Marie gave a tired sigh. "Please be quiet, Winthrop. And Helen is quite right. Once you are married to her there won't ever be any doubt as to the type of woman who bears your name. She'll take good care to advertise it. From the very start people will know."

Helen's color heightened as she snapped, "At least, I've never been a registered prostitute!"

"Of course not, my dear. You have never been that honestly. And now that you bring it up, I might tell you that it was a profession of which I have never been ashamed. It was without pretense or hypocrisy. Although in those days I was innocent enough to think that the only whores were those who openly admitted the fact. Since then I have learned otherwise. There are women like yourself, women who use their bodies only to satisfy selfish whims and give nothing in return. Whether you are married or not makes small difference. You always cheat. Your morals are as bad as your manners, if I may say so."

"Well, *really*—"

Suddenly Marie was inexpressibly weary of the whole sordid business. She wanted only peace and quiet. She wanted a hot, pine-scented bath to cleanse her of the dirt that seemed almost visible in the air.

She stood up and said sharply, "Please excuse me. And please leave quickly. Both of you. This is not a house of assignation. It is my home and the home of my children.

"I prefer to keep it clean!"

CHAPTER TWENTY-FOUR

T HE BOARDMAN DIVORCE was a minor sensation and a topic for speculative gossip for several months in Old Haven.

For one thing, there was the quietness with which it was accomplished. To all intents and purposes, Marie simply departed on a spring cruise, and not until some weeks later, when news of the divorce obtained in the Virgin Islands was printed in the sedate pages of the New York Times and Herald Tribune did anyone realize what was, or had been, in the wind.

There were those who wondered about the suddenness of it, and others who wondered why it had taken her so long to lose patience with Winthrop's repeated infidelities.

But when the divorce was followed almost immediately by news of Winthrop's marriage to Helen Avery gossip and speculation flamed up again.

By then Marie was established once again in her home in Old Haven. The only thing about which most of the local society agreed was that Winthrop had shown a small shred of decency in establishing residence elsewhere.

That was after it became known that he and Helen were taking a year-round apartment in New York.

"And a very good thing!" Mrs. Lockridge, the dowager matron of the older set, declared at the monthly meeting of the Garden Club. "Certainly none of the old families would care to receive either one of them *here.* I think the whole business is in shockingly bad taste. I must say that Marie has handled herself very well through the whole trying affair."

"She always does," Mrs. Grayson reminded. "But then, of course, she's a lady in the true sense."

Mrs. Lockridge sniffed. "Any fool could see that. As my mother used to say, breeding always shows...."

THE END

www.ingramcontent.com/pod-product-compliance
Lightning Source LLC
Chambersburg PA
CBHW052006240626
47153CB00008B/2763